Love Saw It

Love Saw It

Cindy M. Williams

To order additional copies of this book, contact:
Xlibris
1-888-795-4274
www.Xlibris.com
Orders@Xlibris.com
703639

Contents

Love, Leave Or Lose

You could've never told me in a million years that my life would be ending like this. It's 5 a.m. Terrence is in the emergency room and Chad is in jail. How did we get to this point? I never saw it coming! My life was going to damn good for this to happen, but all good things must come to an end. I knew sooner or later a decision would have to be made but I didn't think it would be more sooner than later. I guess doing what I was doing a decision was going to be made by me or the man upstairs, I think I took too long, now I'm in this mess. "Lord if you get me out of this I promise I wont ever make this mistake again".

By the way, my name is Sicily Bryant Robinson. I kept my maiden name in case I ever got a divorce I could drop the Robinson and go back to Bryant. I know it's a terrible way of thinking going into my marriage but what the hell, Im a realist, plus it sounded good at the time and I didn't want to lose a part of me. I am CEO of my own company, 15 stores in 10 different cities, a mother of three, a wife of 21 years and at the age of 40 I look damn good. Take it from me, what looks good on the outside isn't always good on the inside. I guess what I'm trying to say is Terrence is my husband, Chad is my lover and this is how we got here.

Me And Terrence

I met Terrence my senior year in high school. He was a popular football player, a jock as they called him and a very handsome young man. I always knew he would make it someday whether it was football or in business I just knew. We dated all through college and the day before graduation he proposed to me at a friend's party. It didn't surprise me that his frat brothers were involved, they stuck together like glue and was a part of everything the other did, but I have to admit it was sweet. After graduation we both decided to move to Atlanta Georgia and make it our home. We bought a four bedroom, three and a half bath house, he got his Ford truck and I got my Q56. With two great careers and planning a family you would have thought we'd be on our way and live happily ever after, so did I. Over the years I had given birth to three handsome boys that seemed to have grown up right before our eyes. Randall was now 19, Clifford 17, and Terrell was 16. The two older boys were like their dad sort of set in their ways while Terrell took after me. We had a good thing going.

Randall Leaves The Nest

I can honestly say that although I had a great career going I was also very involved in my boys life. Randall had graduated high school and decided to go to Jacksonville State College in Jacksonville Florida. It was a week before his big move and we were doing some last minute shopping to make sure he had everything he needed. "Mom are you sure you're gonna be okay with me leaving and going so far?" I had no idea where that question came from but then again Randall always kept my feelings and thoughts close at heart so it didn't surprise me. I stopped in my tracks and placed my hands on his cheeks, "of course I will, I am very proud of you and I know you are doing the right thing. I'm going to miss you like crazy but I will be fine. Just don't be surprised if you look up one day and I'm knocking on your door." There was no way I was going to tell him I was falling to pieces inside at the thought of my first born leaving the nest but I realized months ago that I had to let them live their lives and become men. I had Terrence and the other two at home to look after and keep me company so I was going to be fine. He laughed at the thought of me popping up and gave me a kiss on the cheek for reassurance. We stopped at the school to pick up Clifford and Terrell who were waiting outside with some friends. They were aware of Randall's leaving and wanted to say their goodbyes. As we drove off they yelled goodbye and told him to keep in touch. I think that is when it became real to Clifford and Terrell that their brother was really leaving in a week so the ride home became very quiet.

Pulling into our three car garage Terrell looked at Randall and asked if he was going to take his car. Without a second thought Randall laughed and said "what would college be without a ride?" We all laughed and walked inside the house. As usual Terrence had not made it home. Then again he never made it home before 7 on Friday. He had pay checks to get out, plans to fax and paper work to finalize. He owned and ran a popular construction company that was becoming the largest in our area so he stayed busy. Six trucks, twenty-four man crew and projects that were booked through the rest of the year. I was very proud of him and he knew it. We discussed every move he made for his business as well as mine. We both were determined to be successful both in the work place and home.

It was a warm Saturday morning in June and we were running around like little school kids trying not to miss their bus when actually we were getting ready to take Randall to Jacksonville State where he already had a job lined up and was starting on Monday. He decided it was his way to get himself settled into a strange place and get some money under his belt. He had promised to live on campus his first three years of school and if he kept a B average or above come senior year we'd help him get an apartment. We were all packed and ready to go.

Terrence and Terrell rode down with Randall in his car while Clifford and I followed. The five and a half drive didn't really seem long. As we arrived on campus it was obvious Randall wasn't the only one with the idea of coming today. We helped him unload his things and got him settled in before taking the family to dinner. Deciding on a seafood place we'd passed coming in didn't take us far from campus. If the food was good you could be sure it would be one of Randall's new eating joints. We were seated in a spot with a nice view of the city, the service was good, food excellent and price unbeatable. It was almost 8 p.m. and we had to get back on the road for home. Terrence and Randall had their heart to heart man to man chat, looking in the rearview mirror while sitting in the truck with the boys I saw Terrence place a white envelope in Randall's shirt pocket with a pat on the chest. I couldn't help but laughbecause I knew it was money. Before leaving the house this morning I gave him a white envelope while loading the car which had money in it also. He had a good head on his shoulder, wasn't into drinking or drugs and had a strong faith and belief in God so I knew he'd be okay. My first born was a college kid or should I say young man. Take care sweetheart, was all I could whisper as we drove off into the darkness.

Chad Jackson

Terrence had been after me about hiring some help for the store in Savannah. Jessica, the woman that had been my assistant manager for five years recently had her first child and decided not to return to work. Being a mother I understood completely so there were no hard feelings. I had gone on this website that posted resume's and found two that I was very interested in so I decided to set up interviews. There was Chad Jackson, 31 years of age, four years of experience out of New York. Then there was Sheila Willis, 42 years of age, six years of experience, one son from Albany Ga. Let me be the first to say Chad had the balls in his corner. He arrived 20 minutes early for his interview in a fresh navy suit. Standing a tall 6'2, 215 lbs give or take, large brown eyes with a hint of gold that sparkled every time he smiled with those pearly whites. Picture Boris Kodjo but darker, know what I mean. The interview went good, he answered everything right and understood I was serious about my business. I interviewed Sheila the next day, although my mind was already made. To make it seem professional on my end, I waited a day then gave her a call informing her of the decision to hire Chad. You can't win them all.

I must admit I was confident about his skills and he had won me over with the interview, but you have to understand the store in Savannah was my baby so I decided to take a week and go there to help him get settled. My secretary made reservations for one of my favorite hotels in the same downtown area as the store which was convenient, not to mention some of the best restaurants and other boutiques were there. I arrived late Sunday evening, drove by the store then headed to check in. The excitement of a new manager, not to mention handsome,

11

must have tired me along with the drive itself. Once in my room I took a long hot bath, rubbed body butter on my very tensed legs and feet and slid under the sheets. Tomorrow was going to be a busy day and I wanted to be prepared.

I arrived at around 8 that morning to check out things for Chad's 9 o'clock arrival. The store was in great shape, clean as usual. I had good help and they were well paid so there was no reason for it to be any other way. Hearing the lock on the door I turned to see him coming in. Looking dapper as ever and smelling like a dream I greeted him with a simple good morning and he did the same in return. Not sure of the cologne he was wearing I couldn't help but wonder if it had the same affect on other women as it did me. You know the scent that makes you weak in the knees and takes your breath away? The tone of his voice made my ears tingle so I had to step back a little before he picked up on my reactions.

We discussed the type of customers that came through, what they expected from us, and what I expected from him. "Mrs. Robinson I aim to please" he said in almost a seductive whisper and at that moment my voice walked out on me. Trying to clear my throat I finally spoke and said "call my Sicily one on one and Mrs. Robinson when in front of others. We are going to be working together this week and I want you to get comfortable enough to ask me anything." Damn I didn't meant to say it like that, I thought to myself and I think he read my mind because as I looked up into his eyes he had a smirk that said he was thinking of other questions that business. "What I meant was ask anything about the business." As he turned to walk away he paused and replied "I understood you completely".

Our day went by fast and he caught on pretty good. It was now 7 o'clock and we were closing the store. Dinner was heavy on my mind and I was wondering if he was hungry also. "Do you have plans for dinner tonight" I asked without a second thought. I wasn't sure if he did or didn't but I was going to find out. "None that I know of" he said walking towards me. Keeping composure I looked him in the eye and followed with "then why don't we end this evening on a quiet note and have dinner together somewhere peaceful and tasty. There is a place on the water front called Karen's that serves the best seafood and wine money can buy". Reaching around my shoulders to turn off the lights and to set the alarm, he agreed on Karen's. I then flipped the closed sign and he opened the door for us to leave.

The ambiance in Karen's was always that of peace and tranquility, not to mention with a little romance. We sat in a booth by the window where our reflections danced on the water. As the waiter approached Chad spoke before I could ask. "How about you do the ordering and I will do the eating". I couldn't help but laugh. A man with a sense of humor was a good thing in my book. He told me to order what I thought was good or something I liked and he'd be more than happy to eat it.

We ordered the blackened salmon on wild rice with the house salad to start us off and a bottle of their popular red wine. The waiter took the menus and promised to return with the drinks. If I have my way by Chrisette Michele was playing through the speakers. Lord why this song. It was my favorite or shall I say one of my favorites and looking at him swaying back and forth told me he liked it also. I wondered if he was thinking what I was thinking, but then again he seemed all business today so I doubt that very seriously. The waiter returned with our meals in a timely fashion and everything was on point. For a minute I didn't think he was going to say anything but he finally spoke. "Great choice Sicily." Hearing him speak my name made me weak. I took a deep breath and just said thanks. The vibration on my phone broke the spell. Thank you Lord. Looking at it showed it was Terrence.

"Hi honey, how are you and the boys?"

"We are doing good, missing my wife but good. How is it going over there? Did she give you a hard time on her first day?" I guess he didn't get the memo about me hiring the male so I politely said "Terrence she is a he and he did very well on his first day".

"Sicily I'm sorry, I thought you hired Sheila. So what are you doing?" I told him I'd decided to get a bite to eat before heading back to the room and even thought of walking along the pier. We said our goodbyes and I promised to call him tomorrow but he insisted on me calling before I went to bed so I agreed. Before I could say I love you the call ended which was typical of Terrence.

The waiter returned to see if dessert was on our minds and we both said no. Dinner was more than plenty. I paid for the check then asked Chad if he wanted to join me for a walk on the pier. He said a walk would do him some good plus he was enjoying my company outside of work. I had no response but was glad of it.

The sound of the water splashing against the bricks and the music coming from the jazz player on the bench set the mood right for a long walk. We strolled along the strip for about thirty minutes then I excused myself. Before going our separate ways he thanked me for the dinner and peaceful walk and also for the opportunity to work with me. I got to my room sooner than I thought as if I floated along the side walk. After a quick shower and looking over some papers I found myself dozing off and decided to call it a night. I reached for the phone and dialed Terrence keeping my word. The phone rang 4 times with no answer. I left a message then said my prayers. The day had been long and my body was feeling every hour.

I decided to sleep in for a little. Let Chad open the store without me and get going on his own. I arrived at the store around 10 o'clock, to find him assisting the sales clerk who was dazing at him. Trust me I understood but I shot her look which told her to be professional. Heading to the back office I couldn't help but get a whiff of his scent. I made it a tradition to take my associates to dinner and give a gift for Christmas. If he stayed around that long it would be my job to find out what his scent was and make sure he had plenty, my gift to him. Haha. Placing my things on the desk I didn't see him standing in the door. "Sicily again I want to thank you for last night. It was a nice welcoming gesture, one that I must return soon", he said smiling. Only he knew what he meant but I was eager to find out. We went over a few more things and I told him of my departure this evening. That I needed to head back home and work on the other stores. He was given every number to reach me and if he had any questions to call day or night. I gassed up the Q and headed home.

Back In Atlanta

Just the typical Monday, same old people with the same old train of thought. No one here has a clue what hard work is. It seems like they just show up to earn a paycheck. You have no idea how many times I have thought of firing my entire staff and start over. The only problem is they know me too well and what I expect. They jus t don't have any spunk. Speaking of spunk I wonder how Chad is doing. He has been on my mind every since I left savannah. I'm sure he's doing a good job. Maybe I need to be honest with myself and admit there was some kind of odd attraction to mandingo. From the smile, smell, touch and the way he was swaying to the music that night at Karen's. I pushed the thought to the back of my mind and carried on with my day.

I arrived home from work as usual around 7. The house was quiet which meant Clifford was on the phone and Terrell was either on the computer or watching television. As for my husband, let's just say Terrence is at work, late again. I understand he is dedicated and wants the best for his family but there is more to life than money and success as I recall him saying. "Success is nothing without someone you love to share it with".

He walked in the door 8 o'clock sharp. The boys and I had just finished dinner and was getting ready to settle in for the night. They were in their rooms studying and I was turning the lights off in the den. "Sorry I'm late" he said leaning in for a kiss. That sentence was getting pretty damn old but if he wanted to play this game I was eager to follow. "No problem honey, all work and no play" I said as I faked the passionate kiss. He went on to tell me of the new job he had to come in that really needed to be done before the end of the year and had to work it in his schedule. As I turned to walk away he came from behind his back with a beautiful dozen of roses, yellow and red just the way I liked them and apologized again. I couldn't resist the flowers so I followed with a smile and another kiss, this one with more meaning. I knew my husband like the back of my hand, red and yellow roses only meant sex was on the menu for the night.

After a hot soak in the tub, I soothed on my favorite lotion by Victoria Don't Tell Nobody and slid on the two piece blue lingerie set that happened to be Terrence's favorite. I sat at the vanity to fix my hair which length was just passed my shoulders, dark brown with locks I always thought were seductive pinned up. I sprayed on just a little bit of Estee' behind the ears and in the folds of the arms, a gentle breeze of it on the twins (hope you got that) and on each thigh. Oh yeah Mrs. Thang was ready. Rising from my chair I couldn't help but turn to get a look at the way the silk and lace boy shorts was covering my butt. This working out was doing wonders, I turned to get a double take and gave myself high five in the air. The matching top that dipped low exposing part of the twins was fitting like a glove. Mr. Robinson was in for a treat. Terrence never had a problem in bed and I knew tonight wouldn't be any different.

When he entered the room candles were lit in every corner, our favorite merlot was on the nightstand, my favorite mix of music was playing in our ear. A little bit of Luther and Kem how could you go wrong? He was looking so good right now. Body still steaming from his shower, the scent of Dolce in the air bouncing from him and silk black boxers, maybe I was the one in for a treat tonight. Sitting in the middle of our bed I wondered if he could hear my heart beat and my kitty purring as loud as I thought I did. While pulling back the sheet he smiled and raised an eyebrow which told me he was more than pleased at what he saw. Placing his lips on mine with a touch that said he wanted me I could feel a rush come over me that took me by surprise. Holding me and caressing me with his strong warm hands made me want to touch back. Running my fingers from his stomach, to his hips and around to his butt made him tremble. Returning the favor he nibbled on my neck, down to the twins and started on his journey. He made sure each breast received the same treatment, nibble hear, suckle there and a gentle squeeze. Moving down to my stomach laying kisses here and there he managed to speak in a deep but breathless voice "baby your body is so soft and inviting, I don't think I can control myself". Little did he know I was not going to stop him from doing that thing he does so well.

I could feel my shorts easing off my hips, I wanted so much to help him but my body wouldn't move. With understanding he looked at me and smiled letting me know he had it all under control. Bringing them down my legs and placing them on the floor made me pant. Crawling back up he parted my legs and licked each thigh, touching every spot I had and those I wasn't aware of I couldn't help but call his name "Terrence" in a whisper I doubt he heard. But the way he paused on the inner side of my thigh and sucked for a little longer told me he heard. Tasting a little bit of honey then covering all parts again he slowly glided himself home. Our bodies moved to a rhythm that wasn't being played but could be heard by only us. The thickness of his shaft filled me well and the length covered every crook and turn. Our moans grew louder as the rhythm got faster. His grinds became deeper as he pulled me to him. I could feel my body heat rise as a strong sensation came over me. Terrence was breathing harder now which told me he was to the point of satisfaction or should I say beyond. He called my name twice as he began to climax, all I could do was hold on and enjoy the ride.

As we laid in each other's arms for about an hour, neither of us saying a word. Finally he rolled over and poured us a glass of wine as we both toasted to once again a job well done. Showering together trying hard not to start something else, he gave me a bath as I did him ever so softly. We dried each other off and turned in for the night.

Chad's Phone Call

Early the next morning we were up and ready to get our day going. Terrence made us breakfast for the first time in months and we all sat down like a real family and broke bread. As we dressed and was headed out the door the phone rang. The caller id said Savannah which only meant it had to be Chad or someone from the store.

> "This is Sicily is everything ok?"
> "Sorry to call so early but I came across a problem this morning" it was Chad and I could hear the worry in his voice so I told Terrence to go ahead and I would call him later. Placing my things on the counter I returned to the call. "What's the problem Chad?" I had to admit it was good to hear from him.

"This morning when I got in I noticed the back door had been opened and I never got a call from the alarm service. The safe was broken into also but the police said fingerprints were left behind. I didn't want to call you with bad news but I knew I had too." He was so sincerer and concerned. I could hear it in his voice.

"No problem Chad, you did the right thing. Make sure you give them all the information they need and I will be there in a couple of days. Fax a copy of the report to my office when you get it so I can contact my insurance company." We said goodbye then hung up. I couldn't believe the alarm company didn't call. Was the alarm set, was he lying about the situation? What do I really know about him? From out of nowhere all these questions popped in my head. I was wrong for

18

thinking this, I checked his background and everything was fine. The alarm company will have to answer some questions before I let this go. My shop in Savannah is my baby and I can't let this go so easily.

I called Terrence during lunch and told him of the incident. He didn't seem worried or concerned all he said was contact the alarm company and see what they say happened then handle it. What the hell was that to say? Sometimes he can be so loving and then other times I could choke the you know what out of him. Needless to say I had to handle it my way and just let him know the outcome.

The next day I called the company to see why no one called the store or contacted Chad about the break in. The owner gave me some lame excuse about not getting the signal and that someone would be out tomorrow to see what the problem was. Did she really think I was suppose to just accept that and let it go, who did she think she was talking too, a damn dummy? Not by a long shot. She can send someone tomorrow if she wants but best believe I was going to be there to greet them so I hope like hell they got their shit together.

I got off early that evening knowing that I had a drive ahead of me and if I finished a whole day of work it would make the drive that much harder. I called Terrence to let him know I would be going to Savannah all he said was "have a safe drive and call him when I get there". I left the boys a note and told him dinner was in the oven. At 2 o'clock I was on the road headed to Savannah. With my favorite cds and a good bottles of water the drive was not going to be bad. I decided not to call Chad to let him know I was coming and that I would just focus on my visit with the alarm company tomorrow. My secretary had made reservations for me at my favorite Inn and also at Karen's. I have to admit some things about my night with Chad I couldn't forget, which is why I chose to have dinner there again.

5 o'clock on the dot I was pulling up to the Inn. The bellhop took my bags to my room as I followed. Familiar faces greeted me with a warm hello by name that told me either they were on their jobs or I came to much. I think it's the first one. The room was cozy as I remembered with my favorite flowers and bottle of wine. On the pillow was a note that read "welcome back Mrs. Robinson". I decided to take a long bath considering I had another hour and a half before my reservations for dinner. While soaking in the tub I couldn't help but think about Chad and what he was doing around this time. A part of me wanted to call

him and invite him while the other part was saying keep your distance before it goes too far. I soaked a little while longer then got out and started getting dressed. The last time I was at Karen's it was later in the evening and the tone was a little different. Maybe the time of night or the company I had made a lot difference but it was still cozy and welcoming. No matter what the atmosphere was I would have dinner and be off to bed. Tomorrow was a big day and I had to be prepared.

Basking In Savannah

My wakeup call came at 6 a.m. on the dot. I told myself I would be at the boutique before Chad to see what had happened and start calculating my damages. I was dressed and out the door before 8, stopped by the bakery to pick up muffins and coffee and headed to my destination. Walking through the door not expecting the welcome I received. Chad was already there, although I didn't see him lord knows I could smell him. This man's scent could melt even the strongest woman and it was doing a good job on this one. I called out to him to let him know I was there. "Chad are you here it's me Sicily". I started walking to the back looking around the store and not paying attention to where I was going. He must have heard me and was on his way to the front because we ran into each other and we both were startled. Knocking me off balance he reached for me as I begin to topple back and quickly pulled me to him. Without thinking I wrapped my arms around him and held on for dear life. Seconds after coming to my senses and realizing what I was doing, I gently pushed away and told him I was ok.

"Sicily I didn't mean to run you over like that. I heard you call out and came running towards your voice", that's what the man said. "Came running", now that was a first in a long time that I've heard a man say that. I can't remember if Terrence ever came running or walking quickly to my beck and call. His voice had so much sincerity in it, I couldn't help but linger on to his last word.

"It's ok Chad I should have been looking in front of me instead of around the store. I was trying to see how much damage had been done". He could sense the worry in my voice and assured me it was wasn't bad as it looked. We had breakfast and started writing down all that had been tampered or destroyed when the phone rang. It was the alarm company calling to say they wouldn't be able to make it today and would have to come tomorrow. I told the owner that if they were not here bright and early in the morning they would hear from my lawyer.

Around 1:30 we were finished with the inventory list and were getting hungry. We decided to close the store and head toward lake. Chad had left earlier that morning and returned with a picnic basket full of goodies and a blanket and asked me to take a drive. So we closed shop, hopped in his truck and were on the hunt for a quiet spot. We found a little spot away from everyone near the water and decided to post camp between two large boulders. He placed the blanket on the ground then to my surprise he reached down removed my shoes then held my hand as I sat down. Once settled himself he laid everything out nicely and placed a napkin on my lap. He served us turkey sandwiches on wheat with the right touch of mayo, pickles, chips and sparkling water.

"Chad for what do I owe the honors of this treatment" I asked in an innocent voice. "No reason Sicily, I don't need a reason to show how special you are" was his reply. I was taken aback by his choice of words and could feel my palms starting to sweat. I finished my lunch without saying a word but wondered what was he thinking, if anything. The water was beginning to move in on us so we slid the blanket back and sat back down. We had no clue how much time had passed but with the sun turning a beautiful dark orange almost red gave us a clue. I reached down to rub my feet, standing on them day after day in those high heels of mine were now paying off. Chad noticed my pain and asked if he could be of some assistance. The touch of his hands to me back to the very first moment I had been lucky enough to feel them. He massaged my feet as if his hands were made especially for them. The water was still moving in on us but this time he told me not to move and begin cupping the water with his hand and ran it over my feet. Warm and soothing was all I could remember as I enjoyed this special pampering I was receiving. Without thinking I laid back on the blanket as Chad did his thing. I must have dozed off for a minute because I finally realized where I was and what was going on. My skirt was above my thigh and he was running water over my legs.

"Do you want me to stop?" he asked like he knew what my answer was going to be and with an instant I replied "no". My voice sounded as if a frog was in it but again I couldn't believe what was going on. By now he had made it to my thighs and every ache and pain I had ever had was no longer remembered. Every muscle he touched and caressed as if there was no tomorrow. All of a sudden a sensation came over me that told me I either had to give in or he had to stop. Looking into his eyes I could see what he was thinking. Damn this man was so powerful he took my breath away. I reached for his hand motioning him to stop, I couldn't do this here, not like this, not now. This was a business trip and it must be treated like one. I lowered my skirt as we packed the basket. He carried my shoes in one hand and the basket in the other. On the drive back to the boutique we listened to a slow groove by India Arie. It was mellow and right on time. He hummed as I swayed my head back and forth. I was wondering how Chad was feeling but I dared not to ask. The fact that he was humming this song and patting his hand on his knee gave me the impression that he couldn't be too upset. Or at least it didn't show.

Back at the shop we walked through one last time, turned off the big lights, locked the doors and left a small light on inside to keep away the vandals or so we were hoping. He walked me to my car to make sure I made it safe. Looking up at him his eyes were a beautiful color, he smile, said he'd see me later and we went our separate ways. Once I reached my room I called Terrence to give him and update but was shocked to Clifford answered the phone. It was always good to hear from my sons. They were my joy.

"Hey mom how was the drive and how is the store" always straight to the point was Clifford. If there was a question to ask he asked it without any hesitation. I told him the drive wasn't bad and the store is going to be fine. The alarm company wouldn't be out til morning other than that everything is good. I never gave my kids reason to worry about anything that was beyond their control, get your school work and learn to be respectable God fearing men and everything else would fall in place, is what I taught them and this they had. He told me his dad was in the shower and would make sure he got the message to call me back. I told him I loved him and ended my call.

I ordered room service and took a quick shower while waiting on my food to come. I wasn't really that hungry after the lively lunch with Mr. Jackson so I ordered a salad and a diet drink to end my day. Two hours had passed when the phone rang so loud it startled me. "This is Sicily".

"Hi babe how was the drive down?" was Terrence's question. I told him as I told Clifford it was good and then I filled him in on the condition of the store and the phone call with the alarm company. He told me not to worry that everything would be ok. We talked about his day and was damn glad he didn't ask about mine. The boys and our schedules for the next few days were the last things on our list of discussions then said good night. I couldn't sleep that night and it was obvious why. My lunch with Chad had played on my mind all evening and from the looks of things over into the night. This head of mine was saying leave it alone and go to sleep, my hormones and curiosity was saying call him. I wondered which side would win. 434-555-7842 was Chad's number I dialed as if it was programmed into my mind. He answered the phone the sound of his voice told me I woke him up. "Hello", he whispered trying to come out of a deep sleep. I told him I was sorry for waking him but we needed to talk. I could hear him clear his throat and it sounded like he was trying to sit up. I told him I didn't want to discuss this over the phone and wondered if he could come over. Being 2 in the morning, I was shocked when he said yes. I had no idea what I really wanted or was going to talk to him about all I knew was I wanted him near and he was on the way.

There was a knock on the door. I looked over at the clock and saw that it was 2:45. Either Chad raced over here or time flew with me waiting on his arrival. I took my time going to the door, not wanting him to think I was eager for him to get here although I was. Opening the door I forgot I was dressed for bed, which meant a short negligee' and fuzzy slippers. There was no time to change so I opened the door and told him to come in. He smelt like heaven and looked fine as hell in jeans. His t-shirt was one of those that fit every inch of his body right. He leaned over, kissed me on the cheek and said in his sexy voice how lovely I looked. I wondered if that was coming from his brain or the body part below. No matter where it came from, it gave me chills.

I poured us a glass of wine and asked him out on the balcony. The night was cool but my hormones had me very warm. Stars were shining brighter than I had ever seen and they danced a dance unlike none other. What was I going to tell this man as my reason for having him over this time of night? A part of me wanted him to start a conversation but I guess he was waiting on me considering I called him over. "Chad I know you are probably wondering why I asked you over this time of night? To be honest I can't believe you at such hour. You were probably asleep and I am sorry for wakening you". He turned slowly in his chair and placed his glass on the table. "Sicily to be honest with you I couldn't sleep for thinking about our day at the beach". He paused for a second then started again. "I tried hard to forget and to tell myself it was wrong and I shouldn't over step my boundaries. You are my boss and I was wrong but I know what my heart and body was telling me but still I was wrong".

How could I follow with what I was thinking and my body was wanting? Then again we are both adults so I figured I would tell him why I called him over and we would go from there so here was nothing. "Chad I haven't stopped thinking about our day which is part of the reason I called you over". Whew that wasn't so bad, now try the rest I said to myself. "When Im near you my heart beats fast and my hands start to sweat, the smell of your cologne drives me crazy and the touch of your hands today made me want you in ways I shouldn't be thinking of". I turned to look at him, to get an impression that would give me a hint of what he was thinking but for some reason it was hard for me to look in his eyes. I sat there for a few minutes with my head down when all of a sudden I felt him rise from his chair and walk in my direction. He reached out for my hand and pulled me slowly to him. Rubbing his hands across my face and removing the hair from my eyes he lifted my chin up to him and made a connection for the first time since I started our talk.

"Chad I am so sorry if I offended you I never meant to". Before I could finish my sentence his mouth covered mine and we kissed. His lips were soft and warm and it felt so good. My lips parted as his tongue entered ever so slowly. His taste was sweet, sweeter than I could have imagined. With my body against his I could feel me wanting him more and more and it was beginning to show. My nipples became erect and ached for his touch. He must have read my mind or felt them on his chest because at that very moment he began caressing them gently but firm. I was getting weak and needed to come up for air. In whatever voice I had left I told him it wasn't right and that we couldn't do this.

"Baby don't tell me this doesn't feel right, please don't stop me now not like this" as he placed my hand on his very erect spot that could be felt through his jeans. This man was blessed and more than one way. I leaned into his chest as he pulled me closer. His has gripped my bottom and lifted me so I could feel his tool on my tingling spot. Right then I went limp and held on tight. "I got you" he said as he lead me back inside. "Sicily if you want me to leave I will and never try this again but if you want me to stay you have to say it".

"Chad what does this say" I asked as I slowly lowered my straps from my shoulders and let the silk piece of material fall to the floor. The look in his eyes told me he wanted it as bad as I did and I was in for a ride. Picking me up in his arms he began kissing me again but this time with more passion and a more type of want. He laid me on the bed and removed the slippers from my feet one at a time. Sweeping his hands from my toes to my thighs made me quiver. This man knew exactly what he was doing and was going to make every moment count. Pulling his shirt over his head gave me the chance to look at his chest. You would have thought each muscle was carved for him so right. He unbuckled his pants letting them drop to the floor. Nothing like a man in silk boxers and oh my, was this brother wearing them right as if he was poured in them. My body wanted him, ached for him and I felt his do the same. He removed his boxers and stood with his hands to his side as if he was saying "this is what I have to offer" and trust me he was offering a lot. I told him I didn't have any protection, this was new for me. He reached for his pants and removed his wallet. Inside was a gold pack with a condom inside. To be honest I was glad because I didn't want him to stop. I wanted him, needed him and I hoped he needed me.

"Sicily I wouldn't mistreat your body in anyway. I respect you and will protect you". Removing it from its wrapper he placed in on the tip and rolled it slowly to the neck of his very promising manhood. "Baby I hope you are ready" he asked as he lowered his body next to mine. I kissed him on the cheek then on the lips and gave him his answer. We cuddled closely and kissed for several minutes. His hands caressed my body and felt all the places I needed him to feel. He fondled my breast with the tip of his fingers until I thought they were going to pop. I could feel myself getting wet and wanting him more and more. Training my side and stopping at what seemed to be one of his favorite spots, my butt, he pulled me closer so I could feel his need too.

"Chad I want you now, I can't wait and I don't want to have to wait any longer". I said before I knew it and I was glad. At that very moment he opened my legs with one hand and fondled my spot like it had never been done before. His fingertips played with my juices as if he was inside of me. Moaning deep in my throat and moving my hips to his beat told him it was time. He lowered his body on mine and entered me gently. His size was large and could tell by my tensing that he had to take it slow. "I won't break Chad" I told him giving him the okay to enter it all. He was happy to continue and filled me completely. The motion he made was that of a snake touching all sides, every inch and then some. I wrapped my legs around his waist making sure he didn't leave until I was ready and held on for dear life.

Looking down in my eyes he finally spoke "Sicily this is like heaven, warm and wet beyond what I imagined, you are driving me wild, I don't think I can hold it much longer" he whispered in my ear as he began moving faster. My hips were moving to his as I squeezed his penis with every muscle I had inside. I couldn't hold on, I was almost on the edge and he was too. "Come with me Chad", I said as I reached up and met his mouth with mine. Our bodies moved in unison as we clung on to each other. We were getting closer to destiny and I didn't want him to stop. His grind was getting deeper, stronger which told me he was near and I wasn't gonna miss it. "Now babe" I screamed as I started to explode. "Im with you Sic" he said in response as we exploded together. It was so strong and intense, magical. He gave my body what it needed and gave my soul what it was looking for. We lay there for a few minutes in that same spot not wanting to forget what just happened. "Follow me my love". I couldn't imagine what he had in store now. I followed him to the bathroom as he turned on the shower and stepped inside. Pulling me in with him, not worrying about my hair, I came at his command. We showered together, me bathing him he bathing me. It was like making love all over again but only with a touch. We finished, dried off and headed back to the bed to dream sweet dreams. Tonight may not have been what I needed in my life but it was what I needed at this moment.

The Morning After

I rose that morning to the smell of fresh coffee, bagels and eggs, side orders of bacon and fresh fruit. As I rolled over there was a dozen of roses on my pillow and a note that said "Thanks for a memorable night". A woman could get use to this kind of treatment I thought to myself. It was 8 o'clock and I knew I had to meet the alarm company at 10. I rushed through breakfast, jumped into the shower, got dressed and was out the door by 9:30. When I got to the office Chad was already busy with work and had everything going. I could feel myself blush as he turned in my direction. "Don't worry my love I am not going to go for a repeat in the store, right now its business". He leaned over, kissed my cheek and got back to work. A part of me was thinking I wanted a repeat but he was right, business is business. I could see he was hard at work and figured I should do the same. He was dedicated and a hard worker and that meant a lot to me. It was almost noon when the alarm company showed up. Two men in uniforms and a company van pulled up and jumped out like they were ready for business. They did the check on the connections in the store and called the office to see if they got a signal. All was good on this end so the problem had to have come from their end. An apology was made and the owner offered to give three months of free monitoring. "No thanks" I told her. "As soon as I get the figures from the insurance company I will be more than happy to send you the bill". She knew she was in a no win situation and accepted it as that.

We continued on through the day as if nothing happened, but it did, something special and we both knew it. I had to break the ice, the quietness was killing me. "Chad I'm gonna say this and be done, last night wasn't only what I wanted but what I needed and I have no regrets so I don't want you feeling guilty or at least I hope you aren't". I went on to tell him that I was heading back home in the morning and would check on him. The look on his face said that he wasn't happy. It was sad but made me feel good. I knew I was going to be missed and that's always a good thing. He looked in my eyes and said that he understood.

We closed the store at 9 sharp and headed to the parking lot. Chad walked me to my car and opened the door "Sicily it was more than just what I needed it was what I wanted also. Don't let this end". He leaned in for a kiss and at that moment I closed my eyes when out of nowhere a car drove by pretty close and blew the horn. I wasn't sure but the person driving favored Terrence but the vehicle wasn't his and he was in Atlanta. "I guess that is a sign that it ends here" I told him and got in the car. He stood in the parking lot as I drove away. There was a slight sadness in his eyes and a touch of it in my heart. The thought of that car shot across my mind for a minute but I shook it off and continued down the road.

Back at the hotel I had 6 calls, 4 from Terrence, 1 from Randall and the other from an unknown caller. I took a shower, packed my bags and called the house. "Hello mom" it was Clifford. We talked about his day, he said Terrell was fast and his dad was out of town checking on a site for a new contract and would be back tomorrow. I told Clifford goodnight and went to bed. As I lay there I thought it was odd that Terrence didn't mention his trip. I also thought of Chad and the look on his face. Had I made a bigger mistake than I thought? Time would tell is all I can say as I dozed off.

Home Again

I decided to stay home from work today. Figure I had a few things around the house I could take care of. Spend some time with the boys and surprise Terrence with lunch. I had been spending so much time on the store in Savannah I really haven't been checking in on the others. An email would be waiting for me from the store in Albany Ny so I knew that was first on the agenda. Kacey and I haven't talked in a while so it deserved my attention. She managed the store there and Brooklyn and did a pretty good job. She wasn't good at staying in touch like asked but the numbers always looked good at the end of the quarter so I gave her benefit of the doubt. I decided to give her a call.

"Sicily's this is Kacey, how may I help you?"

"Hi Kacey, this is Sicily, how is everything going? Have you had any trouble with anything lately?"

"No Sicily everything is fine. Business has been doing real good. There was a huge party here this past weekend. We started advertising as soon as we heard about it and the customers were coming in like crazy. There is also a Red Carpet event coming in next month. Some of the top dogs asked if we could open the store after hours for a private showing. I told them it would be okay and I would get back with them."

"Very good Kacey I haven't been to New York in a minute so I think that would be the perfect time, call me back before the week is over to let me know the dates so we can really get this going. If you need anything call me. Take care and keep me posted." She told me that she would call me by Friday and if anything else came up I'd be the first to know.

I hung up the phone and started thinking of how successful this event could be and how great it would be for the NY boutique. Business has always been good but it's never too good to make a bigger profit. Kacey was a very professional woman, she really knew her stuff but there were times she gave me the impression that the store was hers. Maybe it was just me but I really had those feelings from time to time. Needless to say as long as my business was straight, nothing came up short and I was always the first to know what was going on I was good. At the end of the day I do the hiring and firing.

The morning was swiftly passing by. I looked at the clock and saw that it was almost 11:00. I had to hurry if I was going to be dressed at Terrence's office by lunch time. I jumped in the shower, through on a cute little sexy but appropriate dress and was in my car by a quarter til. I picked up the phone to call him and let him know I was headed his way before he darted out. "Hi Sic, what do I owe the pleasure my dear?" He could be so sweet sometimes and others you would think he was second cousin to the devil. I told him I was on my way to pick him up for lunch and was wondering if he could be outside waiting. For a second I could have sworn I heard him sigh, what could possibly be wrong now? Then he finally spoke "That would be great sweetie only I already have plans for lunch, I'm having lunch with a new client. Can I take a rain check?" I really didn't have a choice, never was the one to make a man do anything and wasn't about to start. "No problem hun, I'll just drop in on Adriane and visit with her. See you tonight when you get in." Before he had time to answer I hung up.

Adriane was my best friend. We'd been friends since we were toddlers. No matter how long we go without hearing from each other we could always catch up as if it was yesterday. She told it like it was, never sugar coated anything and I think that was one of the reasons I loved her so much. Business wise she was smart as a whip. We had a lot in common. I kept her in the hottest fashions and she made sure my layers stayed soft and bouncy or at least the top stylist in her salon did. She had 8 salons in some of the hottest cities and was working on number 9. Our goal was to have salons and boutiques in the same cities and we were accomplishing that.

I pulled in the parking lot and smiled as I saw her through the window on the phone. She had a sassy attitude that made everyone laugh whenever she got mad. I walked through the door demanding to see the owner. Adriane turned quickly ready to enforce her no loud talking policy. "Heffa you were ten seconds from getting cussed out. Where the hell have you been? I haven't seen you in two weeks, no calls no nothing. Don't make me write you out of my will!" Everyone laughed and although I tried not too I couldn't hold it anymore. "Girl you are so crazy, what would I do without you? Let me think, probably stop drinking." Looking at me from head to toe I knew something smart was coming. "So does Terrence know about the little fling you had with your secret lover today? Not everyone can go around looking like that during the lunch hour." My thoughts quickly went to Chad at the mention of secret lover but I brought myself back to reality fast. I told her about my plans for lunch with Terrence and how they were spoiled. She told me not to worry and that she would take me to lunch, so off we went.

We ended up at this nice little bistro down town. It was very popular but for some reason not very busy today, which was good, we could at least have our favorite table. The waiter seated us without hesitation and brought our usual drinks. "I can't believe it's not busy in here, where is everyone?" I was really talking to myself but know Adriane like I know her, she was going to say what was on her on mind. "Who cares as long as we get to sit at our table?" We order our food and sent the waiter on his way. I looked across the room at my best friend to find her with a smirk on her face looking back at me. "What's on your mind A, why are you looking at me like that, spit it out" I shouted in a playful way. She leaned back in her chair and opened that smart mouth of hers. "Now Mrs. Sicily what's going on in good ole Savannah and don't hold nothing back." I told her it nothing, I hired a new manager, he was doing a great job besides the fact broke in the store but other than that he was really only job. Just the thought of Chad made me smile and at that moment she picked up on it. "Oh hell no Sicily give me figures and hold nothing back" she said sitting up straight. "6'2 215lbs give or take, brown eyes golden specks, Boris Kodjo but darker, hard worker and excellent at what he does" is all I could say without longing for him.

"Damn slut I said describe him not put out an ad. Sic do you have feelings for this man or should I say goddess, better yet have you screwed him?" Was it that obvious? "Adriane get a grip you know darn well I wouldn't do that to Terrence, he is my husband." I tried to sound convincing but I don't think it worked. "Sure my sister" was all she said and gave this slick smile. "Besides he is younger than I and he is my employee" like I was pleading a case. "What the hell does either one have to with anything? If you did or didn't at least he can't fire you!" She said all in a minute then threw her hand up for a high five. Of course I didn't put my hand up. Then followed with "all I'm saying is be careful, you never know where Mr. Terrence himself might show up, don't fall in love because you are married and if he is really good get enough for me because Lord knows my well has been dry for a while." We both laughed out loud and gave high five. The waiter brought us our food which was on the money as usual. I told he all about Savannah and started telling her about New York when she interrupted with "you know you can't leave me out, give me the dates and book my flight with yours." And with that said I knew without a doubt that Adriane would be going to New York with me.

I dropped her off at the shop and schedule a long over do hair appointment. I told her I would fill her in on the information as soon as I got all the dates. We said our goodbyes as I drove off. I had an evening to plan with my sons and I wasn't going to let nothing get in the way. Pulling in the driveway I noticed to extra cars in the yard which told me the boys had company. So I figured why not barbeque and let them enjoy the pool. They were all seated in the family room watching a movie or should I say the movie was watching them they were all sleep. Clifford and Terrell along with Carmen, Nicole, Jack and Sam were quiet and breathing heavy. Carmen and Nicole were the boy's girlfriends and Jack and Sam had been their friends since preschool. "Hello everyone, who's up for a barbeque out by the pool?" and with that being said they all lit up and turned in my direction. The boys got the grill ready and sat everything up around the pool while the girls helped me inside. I wasn't sure what time Terrence would be home but hopefully it wouldn't be late. They kids played volleyball in the pool and at snacks while I grilled. Music was played as we all laughed and danced. No matter what kind of day I was having my boys could always turn it around for me and I knew I was blessed.

Chicken, steaks, baked potatoes, tossed salad and grilled corn was the menu. Whenever I got in the mood to cook I always went out that way and I ended with strawberry shortcake. We sat on the patio and ate like it was our last meal. It was seven o'clock and still no Terrence, I thought about calling him but then again he hadn't called me so why should I? The kids helped me clean and put away everything. Being teenagers they all left with food for later. I didn't mind, that only meant less I would have to put in the fridge. They said their thank you and goodbyes and headed out the door.

I put the food away. I figured if he was hungry when he got home he could heat is own damn food up. Heading upstairs I thought about Chad for a second but then I placed him in the back of my mind. I turned the water on in the tub, lit my candles that gave me serenity and turned on the wall unit to listen to a little jazz as I soaked. The bubbles sparkled from the glare of the candles and the water was the right temperature. The scent of lavender filled the room and made me relax even more. I must have dozed off because the water was cold, the candles were burned down and the clock on the counter read and hour later from the time I got in. I dried off, rubbed some moisturizer on my body and headed to bed. I peaked in on the boys and kissed them goodnight. On the way back to my room I heard the alarm ring then set which meant his ass was home. I rushed in the room, jumped in the bed and acted like I had been sleep for a while.

"Sicily are you sleep honey?" I heard him say in a low voice. I could have answered him but I figured why should I. he placed his briefcase in the corner and headed for the shower. It was a quick one that lasted all of ten minutes. He got dressed in his pajamas then went to the kitchen. I stood on the stairs and listened to him heat and eat his food. He cleaned up his mess and was coming my way. I ran, jumped in the bed and pretended to be sleep again. Sliding in bed not trying to awake me, he kissed my back and whispered goodnight. A part of me wanted to turn over but why should I? If sex was what he was after it wasn't going to happen tonight. Maybe if he called or come home sooner he may have gotten some but he didn't and he wasn't.

Planning For New York

Kacey called me bright and early Friday morning with all the information needed. She booked the flights for me and Adriane and made reservations for us to stay at the NY Towers. I told Terrence about the showing and the Red Carpet event that morning during breakfast. All he could say was "good job babe, it should be a hit". He never said anything about going with me for support or a little getaway and I wasn't going to ask his behind either. He said he would be in before late and we would probably catch a movie later on tonight then off he went.

I decided to call Chad to see how things were going and to tell him of the trip to New York. Not as a way of trying to get him to come but to let him know where I would be if anything came up or he needed me and also to be on his p's and q's because I was going to be further way if something happened. I had trust in him and knew he would be fine. The phone rang twice and the sound of his voice made me choke for a second. Flashbacks of us on the beach and in my room suddenly came to my mind as if it were yesterday.

"Sicily's how may I help you?" he said in such a sexy but professional voice. "Hello Chad, this is Sicily. I was calling to check on you and the store and also to inform you that I will be going to New York in two weeks. I will be there four days, leaving that Thursday and returning on Sunday. If by chance you need to contact me for anything feel free to call my cell." I felt as if I had gotten it all out in one breath because I was a little short winded. There was silence for a brief minute then he spoke. "Do you already have your reservations as where you will be staying just in case I can't reach you on your cell?" Look at him trying to be slick. As if I wouldn't catch on. You have to get up pretty early in the morning to fool me but I gave him the info to make him happy. "Yes I will be staying at the NY Towers with my best friend, are you sure that's why you wanted to know?" If he wants to play this game I will be more than happy to help him. "Sure Sic, just wanted to be able to get you when I need you." I also caught on to that when I need you and not if. This man this man. He is not going to drive me crazy. "What is going on in the NY if you don't mind me asking?" Trust me he didn't mind asking.

I told him of the big Red Carp even that Kacey had informed me of and how some of the big wigs wanted a private showing of the store, of course I felt she could handle it but I wanted to be there to add that special touch. Not to mention for the actual event. I couldn't help but wonder if he wanted to go. He wouldn't dare ask me? He said he was just wondering what the situation was and for me to have a good tie. Chad sounded a little sad but I didn't say anything. We said our goodbyes, or should I say see you later, as he put it, then ended the call. Mr. Jackson was a mystery all by himself and I was going to find out more about him. The important things I already knew so we can leave it at that.

I called Adriane to give her the details of the trip and to see when she wanted to get together and do some shopping. Me going to New York, you know there is going to be some shopping before and after I arrive. We decided to cut our days short this coming Monday and Tuesday so we can shop n the city but not all day. I met Adriane at Saks that Monday after lunch. "Looks like we aren't the only ones cutting work today? I hope this means they are having a sale." She said in a whatever kind of voice.

"Adriane there is a price to pay for looking good, just be glad we can pay it." She gave me that whatever look again and continued looking on the racks. We both picked out two hot black spaghetti strap gowns for the event on Saturday night. The accessories we would work on tomorrow. Now that the main piece was out the way we picked up a few other items here and there and decided to call it a day.

"Don't forget I will be in there Wednesday morning for my appointment. Come to work on time ma'am. I don't have all day to wait in you." She always hated when I said that. She would always say what's the purpose of having your own if you cant come when you want? She's so funny like that. Licking out her tongue she peeled off like a bat out of hell. One day that girl is really going to get a ticket, but I hope not.

I stopped at the edge of the drive to check the mail. In it was letter from a rental car place in Savannah. The note said thank you for doing business with us and there was a coupon to use on the next visit. I figured it had to have been a mistake because I drove my car. It was probably somebody trying to score some business. Nevertheless I threw it in the trash with the rest of the junk mail.

Terrence's work truck was in the driveway. It was only 5:30 in the evening and that was early for him. He has to be either up to something or sick. It's rare he gets sick so I knew he was up to something. As I reached the top of the stairs I could hear him rambling through some papers on the desk but as soon as I stepped in the room he dropped them and looking in my direction all startled.

"Baby you scared me tipping in here like that" he said. Who was tipping, I came in as usual. "Tipping like what Terrence, I am wearing heals and trust me I was not tipping, what are you looking for, need me to help you?" He told me no and said he was looking for something pertaining to work. Thought he had left it on the desk last night but probably left it in the truck. He asked if we could go out for dinner and let the boys order in and that he would be ready to leave in an hour give and take so for me to be ready. Gave those orders all in one sentence and didn't wait for me to answer. Is it me or was he acting funny? I know him a little too well, his ass is definitely up to something but what? Only time will tell.

I went downstairs and pulled out the menu book for the boys and called them in to tell them our plans for the evening. The last time they ordered in Terrell chose so tonight would be Clifford's turn. I went back to my room for a quick shower, got dressed, pinned up my hair and waiting for Terrence in the family room. Fifteen minutes later we were in the car headed down town. It was rare that Terrence chose to eat out so I was up for anything tonight. Something about his actions kept poking at me but I didn't let that spoil our evening.

Once seated inside he ordered the wine and our food without even asking me what I wanted. I guess this was his way of being in control for the night so I'll let him have his way. He was always good at choosing our menus and knew what I like so I wasn't disappointed. The waiter brought the wine and our salads. Once he left the table Terrence started to speak. "Sicily I was thinking of taking the boys to see Randall the weekend you are in New York. They haven't seen him in a few months and Jacksonville would be pleasant this time of year. I figured with Adriane tagging along you would be okay and it would give us guys some manly time" Here he was with that fast talking shit of his again. The fact that he wanted to take the boys somewhere was a dead giveaway but I didn't bring it to the table. All I said was "sounds like a good idea sweetie, hope you guys have fun. I'll get a gift pack up for Randall that way you can take it with you. Do you need me to make any reservations?" He answered no real quick like then said he already had some on hold just needed to confirm. They would leave that Friday and return on Sunday. The idea sounded good but something still wasn't right. We enjoyed our meals, danced a couple of songs and headed home for the night.

The t.v. was on in the boys room and they were fast asleep. We got ready for bed, kissed each other goodnight and drifted off ourselves. It was a pleasant evening one I really enjoyed so I was at peace.

Off To The Ny

The morning of our departure I made sure the family had everything they needed and that Randall's gift was in the truck. Terrence gave me the "I'm going to miss you speech and call me if you need me and to make sure I called when I got to the room". I kissed him and the boys, got in the cab and was headed to the airport to meet Adriane. For once she was on time and made it there before me. The last few trips we've made I was the first one to arrive and always had to wait a little more than 30 minutes but not today, Ms Thang was on it.

"I thought I was going to have to leave you and meet you in New York, girl you are slower than Christmas" she said before I could get out. The fact that she beat me here told me I was going to hear about this the entire trip. But this was Adriane so did I expect any different and it was funny hearing her ramble on like that. "Sorry madam, didn't mean to keep you waiting" I told her in a sarcastic way and we both laughed. The driver made handed our bags over and we boarded the plane. She always had to have a window seat and this time wasn't different. The flight was calm and quiet. No nagging little kids or crying babies so I was more than happy. A little over an hour we landed and had our feet in the Big Apple. A driver had been hired for the entire weekend so he was there waiting with a sign that read "Sicily Robinson". He greeted us, tipped his hat, told us the bags were already in the car and lead the way to the limo in waiting. I told my bestie I was sure she wanted to get to the room and take a shower to freshen up but if we could make one stop the rest of the evening would be hers. She gave me this don't push it look but smiled in agreement.

As we pulled in front of the boutique it looked a little crowded for this time of the day but who was I to complain. I could see Kacey from the window working her butt off as usual. A sales associate noticed us getting out and brought it to Kacey's attention. She met us at the door all smiles and open arms. She had the store lit up with a red carpet all rolled and in the corner for our morning showing. She was forever on point with things and had a very creative mind, she was definitely a keeper and if I wasn't careful a little competition if she every stepped out on her own. We talked over plans, walked through the store and discussed what time we would meet back here in the morning. In less than an hour we were back in the car and headed to our room, didn't see any need to hang around she had everything in order.

They welcomed us at the New York Towers as if we were there often. I know it's sad to say but the last time I was there was over a year ago, so the welcome we got actually made me feel good. Once we were settled in our rooms we made plans to order in, get a nap and then get dressed to go out on the town. Room service was there within thirty minutes and before I knew it I was stretched across the bed dozing. Before going into a deep sleep I jumped up to check on Terrence and the boys and to call Chad but at that very moment there was a knock on the door. When I opened I couldn't help but smile at the delivery guy holding a bouquet of flowers and a bottle of Chardonnay. I gave him a tip then closed the door, excited about reading the card. Seated back on the bed I was surprised to see all of this was from Chad. I figured it would've been from Terrence but I was happy. The card read "Hope your visit is what it needs to be, have a wonderful weekend . . . missing you." By the time I was able to put the card down and the flowers to my nose I got a call from Adriane next door. "I saw that shit and I know damn well they are not from Terrence, girl you must have rocked that tenderoni's world, just wanted to say that now I'm going back to sleep. Heffa" and hung up before I could say a word. Placing the items on the bed I decided to go ahead and make my calls so that I could get a nap and be fresh for the night. As I dialed Terrence phone I realized by the third ring that he was not going to answer. I figured all was okay considering haven't heard otherwise so I left a message asking him to call. The next call was to Chad Jackson before the second ring could finish he was on the other end. "Hello beautiful, how was your flight and did you get your welcoming gift?" in a low key type voice. I told him I had, the flight was pleasant and my gift was wonderful. I told him my plans for the weekend, that we were going out later and I would have my phone with me if he wanted to reach me. He laughed and replied that he wanted to reach me but not by phone. I couldn't help but blush and agree. We said our see you later and I was back on the bed.

After a good shower and getting dressed, I called Adriane and told her to meet me in the lobby. Getting off the elevator and looking at her, we couldn't help but laugh. Our black dresses were similar and so were the shoes. The accessories were different as usual. She was always the one to take a chance with hers while I played it safe needless to say we looked like a million bucks and coming from the looks we were getting I was willing to place a bet. The driver was waiting outside on time and held the door for us to get in. I told him we were going to the Bird on 34th street and he quickly headed in that direction. Tall buildings big lights and lots of traffic was the scenery for the night. It was New York so what did you really expect. I looked over at Adriane as she clicked her heels and said "there's no place like home, there's no place like home." I couldn't help but laugh at her silliness. She always made me laugh which was a good thing, laughter is good for the soul. We arrived at the club in all of twenty minutes. It was crowded with a long line outside. We were on VIP so I wasn't worried about the wait. "Good evening Mrs. Robinson, Ms Baker, as always good to see you" the owner of the club said as he met us at the door. "We have a special table for you waiting on the second floor so you can look out. If you need anything else please let me know and enjoy your night." As he turned to walk off Adriane looked at me and said "nice."

The club was packed as usual, ladies dressed to the nine and fellas were fly. One thing about The Bird, no one came in that wasn't properly dressed and to the fullest. The dj was bumping New York by Jay-Z and Alicia Keys so of course the dance floor was packed. I think even those that were not from New York was trying to represent, funny. As two guys approached our table my phone started to vibrate, looking at the screen I could see it was Terrence, on cue as usual. "Hey sweetie, sorry I haven't called earlier. Randall took us on a tour of campus then to his favorite eating spot then off to meet some friends, did you know he was dating or should I say has been dating someone since his second week here? He didn't waste any time, what is all of that noise in the background?" In one breath he said all that before I could get a word in or even think of answering but I jumped in. "That's good dear, no I didn't know that and we are at The Bird." I figured I better say all I can while I can. The phone was quiet for a second which told me he was not pleased with me being out but it wasn't something he couldn't get over. He told me they were getting ready to turn in and would call me tomorrow. We said I love you and ended the call.

I looked up to find the two guys still waiting, are you serious. I really thought they would've been gone boy was I wrong. "Sic this is Donnie and Clyde." Adriane said with a very crazy look on her face. I thought she was joking as she said that but looking at these clowns smiling told me she was for real. Trying to keep my composure I shook their hands and said hello. They asked if we wanted to dance and I politely said no. I couldn't wait for them to leave before breaking out in laughter. No matter where you go there will always be some jokesters over your shoulder, I guess they were ours for the night. Although we didn't dance with any men, we did our usual stepping to our favorite song and then headed out the door. Our day had been full and busy so we were ready to call it quits. As we approached the car the driver handed me an envelope and said the bouncer delivered it to him. While riding back to the room I decided to open it. Inside was a short letter that read "hope your visit here is pleasant, enjoy but be careful." The look on my face told Adriane that something was wrong. After reading the note she asked me who was it from. There was no name just a plain envelope. She told me not to worry, it was probably from the guys we turned down. I stopped by the front desk to see if there were any messages, the clerk told me no but said there was a lady that stopped in but didn't leave her name. I wasn't sure who that could have been. Kacey would have called my phone if she needed me and no one else here knew I was in town, or so I thought.

Riding up on the elevator Adriane asked if something was going on that I wasn't telling her and to be honest. I told her about the almost kiss with Chad in Savannah and the car getting too close. She said it was my conscious getting the best of me and we really had to talk about that weekend. As I told her everything all she could do was say ooh and ah and go girl do your thing and ended with "Terrence will kick Chad's butt if he ever found out, talk about benefits on the job." We both laughed and went to our rooms. Although I was tired I couldn't stop thinking about the letter which also kept me going back to the car in Savannah. Maybe my mind was playing tricks on me then again maybe not.

I was up and ready to head to the store by 8:30 sharp. Adriane on the other hand was just getting up. I told her I would head out and send the car back for her in a few hours. A morning per she was not. Kacey was already there with books laid out for that last viewing and all models there for their last reminders. Tonight was going to be a big night and meant a lot of things for everyone involved so it had to be right. Adriane and I had shopped for our outfits back home but were going to get a glance at some stores in New York before making our final decision. A few of the top stores had set aside rooms in the back for us to take a look at things in our size. Something was bought from each store by us both which we knew would happen. We decided on what to wear grabbed some lunch to take back to the room and waited for our private 4 o'clock massage, mani and pedicure. In the room were a dozen of roses, 11 red and 1 yellow in the middle. How sweet of Terrence, I thought as I reached for the card but was shocked to find they were from Chad. Adriane snatched the card and chuckled as she read it. "Someone has a brother hooked," she said while doing her little dance she does when she is being sassy.

"No one is hooked he's just being nice and concerned of his boss. He knows how important tonight is for me and what it means to my stores and me. Don't trip chick you know also. Although I am surprised they aren't from Terrence. It almost pisses me off to know that he hasn't called and wished good luck or anything."

"Don't worry girl I gotcha and if I don't looks like Chad does, Mr. Jackson if you're nasty." I couldn't help but laugh as I walked to the door. Our pamper party was on time and were good and ready to be pampered. Once on the table my girl Adriane was the first to speak. "I am so glad they sent men and not women for the massages. I would rather have a man rub me than a woman any day. As for the nails ole girl can do them all day." Ha ha. "I feel you on that girlfriend. Chad has wonderful hands. Oops." It slipped before I knew what hit me but of course she caught every word. With her head spinning like magic she looked at me all buck eyed. "I want every word or should I say every touch and this time tell me the truth, the whole truth." As before I told her of our evening but I did leave out the love making part and the part about the shower so I guess I owed her the truth. She is my best friend and we have shared so much.

I told her of the magical night that we had and how much of a gentleman Chad was. The passion we shared before during and after. Every word was with a sigh or a smile just thinking back on the night. She looked at me in shock and never said a word the entire time I talked. For her that was a first so I don't know if that was good or bad. Once I was quiet, all she said was "damn". She never asked about Terrence or what I was going to do or if it was going to happen again. To be honest her being speechless made me wonder but I soon got over that moment when I looked at the clock. We had to be on the red carpet for our walk at 8:00 and it was almost 6. After the quick drying of the nails we both tipped the helpers and showed them to the door. Adriane returned to her room as we showered, did our hair and makeup, got dressed and was downstairs waiting for the car at exactly 7:15, perfect timing.

Red Carpet

As we pulled up to the event of the evening or should I say the month bright lights were circling the sky, the cameras were flashing and every magazine and newspaper had their representative there getting all the news and pictures. Once on the carpet with Adriane on my left and Kacey on my right I became nervous. I think they both sensed it because at the same time they leaned in and said "You will be fine, you look great." I smiled and thought we look great. Half way down the carpet the high spirited speak your mind Wendy Williams was there as always in the right place when something big is going on asking all the right questions, whether the timing was right or not. When Wendy is in the house your butt better be ready for anything and if there any bones in the closet you better lock the door so they don't fall out. This sister does not play. I saw her approaching so I went straight to her. "Hello Sicily Robinson how are you doing tonight?" She started off all sweet but I had a feeling something slick was going to follow. "I'm feeling great Wendy and you?" I returned it. "Good and who do you have with you and where is your husband?" She started to laugh. "This is my good friend Adriane and my right hand Kacey and my husband is in Florida with our sons. As far as the business, the jewelry is flashy and the fashion is fly as always. Hope you enjoy your evening." I said all that in one breath to keep her from getting off the issue of the night and out of my personal life. We walked with a good stride down the carpet, stopping here and there and what seemed like an hour we finally made it to the entrance and to our table. There was an elegant table for 8 waiting for us as we were seated. There were going to be some models tonight, each brought a guest and then there was us. Other people in the fashion industry were their making their mark and networking.

The models were great as usual. I always used the same ones whenever a showing was coming up or I did an advertisement. They have yet to let me down which made my job a little easier far as preparing for these events. Awards were given out and I must say I was little shocked when we won top boutique of the year. I took my entire table up there on the stage as I accepted the award, said a quick dedication to God Almighty, my family and my staff and friends. The night slowly came to an end and my feet were killing me. Being sexy and smiling all night in a 5 inch hill was no play thing but we did it well.

The ride back to the hotel was quiet. We'd accomplished a job well done and now we were ready for some shuteye. I didn't check my messages although I saw the phone flashing. Whoever it was would have to wait til morning. I knew it wasn't Terrence or the boys because they had my cell number so a few hours longer wouldn't hurt whoever it was. We were dressed, packed and heading for the airport at 7:45. Our 9 o'clock flight would be boarding soon and I hate standing in line. Adriane and Kacey both thanked me for a wonderful but busy weekend and I in returned thanked them. I couldn't have done it without them. They were the greatest. We took our seats in first class and enjoyed another crying childless flight.

Home Sweet Home

Pulling in the driveway I noticed Clifford and Terrell waiting on the porch. It always made me smile to see my family. They were the glue that held things together and pushed me forward. You are supposed to want better for your kids than you had. I can honestly say I had a great childhood I made sure my babies had the same. Any sight of Terrence was not to be seen. Considering it was a Sunday the thought of him working was out the question. That was one day he didn't work so I will give him the benefit of the doubt and say he was running errands or visiting friends.

The boys removed my bags from the car and took them to my room. They were so anxious to tell me of their visit with Randall and how much fun they had with his friends. They told me each and every hour of their weekend so it seemed which was good. I did notice that the events for their Friday night did not include their dad. Maybe he let them hang out with the guys and stayed back in the room on the phone handling business. Who knows?

We ordered in considering the busy weekend we all had. As we sat around the table Terrence steps in and decided to join us that last few minutes of dinner. The boys were excited about my award. Lots of questions were asked as far as that night was concerned and like always they wanted to know whom I spoke with and who was there. "Mom you better be glad Wendy didn't have anything to put you on blast about. She is so good about that kind of stuff" Clifford said then we all laughed. All except for Terrence, but I did hear him say "yeah right." What he meant by that is beyond me but I was not concerned. My bed was calling me and I was eager to answer. Once upstairs it donned on me that I never checked my messages before leaving the hotel this morning. I quickly called Kacey and had her to have the hotel forward them to my phone, told her goodnight and was sleep before Terrence could even hit the sheets.

The sound of Terrence alarm clock going off always woke me before I was ready but that was no concern of his. "Just because you have to be up at 6 means I have too? Remember I don't have to be open til 10 and even then there is always someone there to open for me" the words blurted out before I knew what hit me.

"Excuse the hell out of me Mrs. Sicily Robinson, my bad Sicily Bryant Robinson wouldn't want to disturb the queen." I couldn't believe the tone in his voice or the choice of words. He had never talked to me that way and I really couldn't understand his reason for this now. "Terrence I don't know what your problem is or why you have been cold to me lately but if there is something we need to put on the table by all means let's get it out. I am your wife and you are not going to talk to me like one of your employees!" He looked at me with this strange look in his eyes. Never saying a word he picked up his briefcase and was out the door.

Two hours later I was up getting dressed. I fixed the boys and me breakfast and headed up to the office. The Atlanta store was my home so this is where I combined two rooms in the back and made it my office. It had everything I needed right there and also gave me the opportunity to keep an eye on things. Once settled in I decided to check my messages. The first five were from people at the show saying congratulations and let's get together to network. Two of the calls were from Chad calling to check on me and how things went and also to tell me that he caught the live interview on the carpet with Wendy Williams and how well I handled it. The last call was weird and the voice was one I couldn't catch. At first the caller held the phone for a few seconds and then they said in a strange voice "I guess the night belongs to you but not everything is yours." Out of all the messages I decided to keep this one. I called Adriane and played it for her. Once again she asked me had I stepped on any toes recently and again the answer was no so we left it at that and made plans for lunch.

We decided to meet at our favorite spot but this time we picked a different table. The waiter couldn't believe the sudden change. That table had been ours ever y visit for the past two years but today I felt the need for change and I think the message had something to do with it. We ordered our signature salads but decided against the drinks and instead we had water with lemon. Adriane could tell there was something on my mind so there was no hesitation in asking. "Tell me what's on your mind girlfriend."

"Girl I'm not going to lie that message got to me. It made me think about the letter from the club and for some reason it goes back to the morning after that I had with Chad in Savannah." I wasn't sure if on e had something to do with the other but nothing else like that had ever happened.

"Sweetie I think it's your imagination for one and as far as the note and the message that's probably some envious ass nut that's scared my girl is about to take over and put their stores out of business. Don't worry I got your back. Have you told Terrence of these mishaps" she asked.

"To be honest no I haven't, he woke up this morning with his ass on his shoulder being all rude and selfish so I didn't tell him anything after we had a few words. I really thought he would have called me for lunch to apologize but guess he wasn't concerned about what was said or if it hurt my feelings." The Terrence I know would have flooded my office with roses and lunch followed by makeup sex would have been first on his agenda. The Terrence that walked out this morning without saying a word was a stranger to me. Maybe it would all come out soon. We finished our lunch and headed our separate way. Adriane promised me everything would be okay and I believed her but something also told me that there would be some rain before the sun but I would be read for what was to come.

Terrence and I arrived home at the same time for a change. He helped me prepare dinner. The conversation around the table was short but sweet. I did my best to keep the boys from detecting anything. Whatever the problem was Terrence and I would fix it and not involve them. Our problem was just that, our problem. The boys agreed to clear the table and do the dishes so I kissed them goodnight, checked all the doors then headed upstairs to bed. I took a quick shower, wrapped my hair and was sleep in minutes. Not sure of how long I had been sleep the feel of Terrence shaking my shoulder brought whatever dream I was having to an end. "Baby I am so sorry about this morning. I should have said something sooner but my pride stood in the way, hope you can forgive me?" I turned over gave him a kiss and told him to forget it. We sealed it with a kiss then went back to neutral corners of the bed. In the back of my mind I wanted to tell him so bad "next time your pride will have your ass on the sofa downstairs" but I kept that one to myself then drifted back to sleep. We'll see what the morning brings.

Instead of waking me up with his alarm clock I was awaken instead with coffee and muffins and a rose. "Thank you so much sweetie, what's this for?" I figured I go ahead and the start the conversation rolling. I know he is up to something. "No reason really, I know I have been a little mean to you lately and figured I would try to make up for it. I am truly sorry." I smiled at him as if I truly believed that but this is Terrence we are talking about, I have been with him for twenty years so I know something is about to follow this sad ass excuse. Right when he was almost done getting dressed he hit me with "babe there is something I need to tell you" as if I didn't know it was coming. "I think I may have a job to do in North Carolina but before I take it I am going up there with one of my guys to look over the area." I may be wrong but it felt like there was more to that than what he was putting on. He has gone on jobsites before and never found it hard to discuss or played the kiss ass game either. "Sure no problem, when are you going and for how long?" I asked. He told me he was thinking on going when I go to Savannah so we would be away and back home at the same time. Red light red light, sound the alarm. This brotha has never ever planned our business trips together now all of a sudden you want to act concerned about our time apart. Yeah right.

We decided to leave the coming Wednesday and return on Sunday. I made flight and hotel arrangements for them in the Carolinas and hotel arrangements for me in Savannah. I check with the boys to see what their plans were for the week to make sure they would be fine and of course they were. They have really grown to be respectable dependable men and sometimes I guess I do treat them like babies. Then again they are my babies. The next couple of days I took care of some unfinished business, made phone calls and checked on Terrence's plans. My arrangements had already been confirmed and the boys were good to go.

For some reason I got up before the alarm could sound. Terrence was slowly moving but as if there was no plane for him to catch but I figured if he wasn't worried, neither was I. As I placed my bags in the car it hit me that I never called Chad to let him know I was coming. I guess that was a good thing. It would give me the opportunity to sneak up on him and see if he is as accurate with his time while I'm away as he is when I'm there. I had my motherly talk with both Clifford and Terrell warning them of house parties and sleepovers while we were away and especially girls. We had raised them to be good men so I trusted them, but then again they were teenagers and with both parents out of the house anything was possible. It was our first time leaving them alone without adult guidance so I was a little on edge. My neighbors were aware of us leaving and said she would check on them from time to time and their grandmother was only half an hour away so they were good. Terrence finally came down with his bags in his hands still walking a casual slow walk. His meeting with the property owner was not until tomorrow so I guess if he missed his flight there was always the next one. As I told them all goodbye and got into my car I noticed Terrence didn't come down with his briefcase. He without his briefcase is like a baby without a bottle, lost. He carried it everywhere we went even if he was off just in case something came up. Maybe he left it in his truck last night or would run back up and get it. No matter what he decided my plans were to be in Savannah by 12 noon and considering it was 8 and I still had to gas up I was going to be on my way.

Back To Savannah

The drive to Savannah was always peaceful to me. Although today's weather was cloudy and full of rain this ride was no different. After driving for two hours I decided to stop to a store to use the restroom and get something cool to drink. While waiting in line my mind suddenly went to Chad. What was he doing and what would he say when he saw me. A part of me wished I had informed him of my arrival. I didn't need any surprises that would make him look bad in my eyes but would that be possible. He always knew what to say, what to do and how to act. A little too good if you know what I mean. Getting back in my car I noticed a dark colored truck in my rearview mirror. The rain was still falling heavy so I couldn't tell if it was dark blue or black. The windows were tinted very dark so whoever was in there was kept a secret. Maybe they were waiting on me to move so they could get my parking space so I buckled up and pulled off.

With less than 15 minutes away from city limits I decided to go by the boutique first before checking in. I knew Chad would be leaving for lunch soon so I wanted to catch him before he left. There was a nice crowd inside so I was very pleased. Our new sales associate had her hands full at the register while the others assisted on the floor. I spoke to them all quietly not to draw any attention from the customers and headed straight to the back. As I approached the office I could hear Chad in an uproar with someone on the phone. This tone of voice coming from him I have never heard before and wouldn't want him to use with me. I couldn't hear the entire conversation but I heard the words like "over" and "never" used several times then he slammed the phone down. I walked in the office as if none of it was heard and he put on a smile that could melt an iceberg. "Sicily, I had no idea you were coming. Why didn't you call and tell me?" He did look a little shocked, well a lot but his words never skipped a beat as he stood up to greet me. I was looking for him to shake my hand or just continue with his conversation of why didn't call but before I could start we were embraced in a two minute hug but felt like hours. I really didn't see that coming so I was the one surprised. We talked a little about the sales and the new items we had received. He still didn't mention the phone call he just had so that told me it wasn't my business. We decided to meet for lunch at 1:30, which would give me time to get checked in and take a quick shower. There was something about Savannah that was always refreshing to me. No matter what time of day it was you always got a good breeze that gave you a second wind. The service at the hotel was one you could always depend on from the time you checked in to the time you checked out. I headed straight to the room and didn't stop til I hit the shower. The ride had been nice but I was getting tired and knew the shower would perk me up plus seeing Chad gave me a spark.

We decided to have lunch at this little bistro that sat beside the ocean. The wind was blowing just right, the weather wasn't too hot and the crowd was nice. I think I saw Chad drool as I walked up. I chose to put on a yellow sundress with spaghetti straps, matching open toe sandals with a low heel but not too low, at least I made my legs look good. My hair was pulled up with a few curls flowing around my face and makeup that was perfect. The dress was made of soft satin that flowed with the wind each time my body moved. Come to think of it I see why he was drooling. I could help but smile as I approached the table. Chad was wearing the same suit he had on at the store but decided to remove his tie unbuttoned his shirt a little and his jacket was lying over the arm of his chair. "Breath taking Sicily" he said in his silk voice. "Thanks Chad, you seem to have all the right word at the right time" I replied. After placing our orders I begin telling him about New York, the award, the letter and back at home with Terrence. He was very proud of my accomplishments and couldn't believe how my husband had carried on after a great weekend. After talking almost an hour about Terrence and me we ended that conversation. I wanted to know about the store and how well it was or wasn't doing.

"So Chad tell me about my baby, is she doing good, how are sales and most important how is the help?"

"Your baby is doing well, sales are great and the help is awesome. They are really pulling their weight and helping out as much as they can. Working late is never a problem if I need them too." I was so glad to hear that. Sometime it can be very hard to find good help and this I know from experience. He continued before I could get a word in edge wise. "The new merchandise was a hit the first week we put it out. Trust me Sicily everything is good on this end, no worries I promise." At that moment he reached out and caressed my hand then held it for a minute or two. He looked into my eyes with this deep mesmerizing look as I looked into his. The waiter broke the spell as he approached our table carrying the food and I was glad he did. I told myself this trip was strictly business and I was going to do my all to keep it that way no matter how sexy Chad is.

"Can I get someone desert or coffee" the waiter asked as he cleared the table. I was stuffed so I knew it was out of the question for me. "Nothing from your desert menu for me either, although I would love to have something sweet." I almost choked when I heard that coming out of Chad's mouth. Looking up at him I could feel him staring at me. He had a smirk on his face that told me exactly what he was thinking, but just as I said earlier, that was not going to happen. "Well Mr. Jackson I won't keep you any longer, lunch time is over I'm sure besides I need to get back in the room and make a few calls. I'll be back at the store before you close." We walked quietly to the corner. I was going left and he was going right. Just as he stepped down to cross the street a dark colored vehicle came flying by and almost hit him. "Chad watch out!" I yelled as I ran to him. Quick thinking made him jump back as the truck approached. He stumbled fallen to the ground. People in the area started running to him asking if he needed help or wanted them to call 911. A gentleman from the bistro stated he tried to get the tag number but there wasn't one. Someone must have called for help anyway because in what felt like seconds the ambulance and police was pulling up together. A report was given to the police and Chad was carried to the hospital just in case the fall had caused an injury. I hurried back to the hotel to retrieve my car.

The hospital was a few miles away but traffic was heavy which made the drive seem longer than it really was. I pulled into the emergency exit and had the security guard to park my car, with a fee of course. "I'm here for Chad Jackson" I told the lady at the front desk. "Are you family ma'am, we can't just give out information" she had this look on her face that told me this chick wasn't playing. "I'm his boss we were together when the accident happened" I hate having to explain as if I was pleading a case. Just give me the damn info is what I wanted to say but figured I better not. She told me the doctors were checking him out and would come to speak with me soon.

I took a seat in the waiting room and started thinking about what just happened. There was something very familiar about the truck then it hit me. It was the same one that was at the store outside the city when I made a potty break or was it? I really didn't know what color the truck was earlier but I knew for a fact this one was black. Was the driver not paying attention when they had come close to hitting Chad or was it done on purpose? Just the thought of it gave me chills. I didn't hear the doctor walk up so it really startled me when he touched my shoulder. "Mrs. Jackson your husband is going to be fine, we are going to keep him for observation til morning but I'm sure everything is fine." Ms Jackson I thought to myself, "Sorry doctor, my name is Sicily Bryant Robinson, I am Mr. Jackson's boss not wife" he said his apology, gave me the room number and told me I could go see him. Although the doctor said he was ok just a little banged up I still didn't know what to expect. Chad was lying in the bed with a monitor and I.V. hooked up. I guess the sound of the door opening woke him up cause when he turned towards me he had this dazed look on his face. "Chad I am sorry this happened to you, are you really ok? How do you feel? Is there anything you need or anything I can do" I was full of questions and decided to take a breather. He reached for my hand pulled me to him and said "just you being here is all I need" then turned his head and went to sleep.

I figured while he was asleep I would run to the boutique to let everyone know what happened to him and close the store down. Everyone sent their get well soon and promised to hold things down while he was out. I wasn't for sure when he would return so I left Kim in charge. I picked him up a few things I figured he would need. I wasn't sure what size he wore so I just guessed and hoped I was right or at least close. I went by the hotel to check my messages and to shower and change. There were 3 messages on the phone. 1 was from Terrell 1 from Adriane and the other from Randall. I returned the one from my son and figured the other two could wait til later. My oldest son was just checking on his mom and wanted to know how things were going here in Savannah. I told him how well sales were and the events of the day. I was still puzzled of the accident involving Chad and wanted to get to the bottom of things. I packed my things in the car and headed back to the hospital. On the drive there I called Terrence to see how things were going with him and his project. He didn't really go into details but hinted around here and there of what was going on. The call lasted every bit of 5 minutes, I love you and then hung up.

I met the nurse in the hallway coming out of Chad's room and asked how he was doing. She told me he didn't eat much but was drinking his fluids well and if there was anything he need to let her know. I entered the room quietly not sure if he was sleep or not but was happy to see him sitting up in bed watching tv. "Hello beautiful, I was wondering where you had gotten off to, hoping you didn't leave me here with these crazies." Although he was dressed in a hospital gown he still looked wonderful. "I went by the store to inform everyone of what was going on they said to tell you hello and take care everything is under control. I also picked up some personals for you hoping the size is right" giving him the bag I gave this teenage blushing smile. He pulled out the items in the bag and laughed when he got to the boxers. I told him I remember seeing boxers on his bottom and not to get any ideas. We both laughed for a few seconds wondering what the other one was thinking. The entire day was like a puzzle and we were trying to piece it together. He asked me to describe the truck and the driver and if I thought it was the same one that I saw at the store. I told him there was some resemblance but I wasn't sure. We also wondered if it had something to do with me or someone I was involved with. We talked for a few minutes then decided to call it a night. Chad had a room to himself but was equipped for two so I got to sleep in the bed next to his. I went into the bathroom to change into sweats and a t-shirts. I pulled my hair back into a ponytail and put socks on my feet. "Damn girl you even look good in sweats and that's not common, when are you not looking good?" This man was one of a kind and I couldn't believe he wasn't married or involved. Then again that could have been who he was arguing with on the phone earlier today. If there was someone special I am sure I would find out soon. The holidays were coming up and I am sure he would want to spend some time them. I picked up my phone to call Adriane, right off the bat she started fussing "why couldn't you answer your phone heffa what have you been doing and why did it take so long to call me back?

I'm waiting." I couldn't help but laugh at her, she always had a way of turning something bad into something good or funny. "Well if you should know I am at the hospital with Chad. Someone tried to run him over today or at least we are hoping that it was an accident." I gave her detail for detail from beginning to end. "Girl I can't believe that. Are you guys okay over there or do I need to come and protect you." Knowing her like I know her she was not playing and would be on the first thing smoking if I needed her to be. I told her we were okay and that I may be down here a little longer than I had planned. I thought about my conversation with Terrence. When I told him what happened all he said was he hoped Chad was fine and to let him know what my plans were as far as returning. There was something weird about the conversation. He spoke on the area of the accident and I don't remember telling him where. I finished my conversation with Adriane then turned off the lights and went to bed.

It was around 4:30 in the morning when I heard Chad moan and turn over in the bed. I got up turned the lights on went to his side. "Do you need something for pain or is there anything I can do for you?" He pulled me closer to him and held on without saying a word. I stood there for a few minutes then moved away. The grip he had tightened as I moved so once again I stood still. He looked so helpless lying there. I felt sorry for him and wanted to do whatever I could to make him feel better. As soon as his grip loosened up I eased away. I slipped on my shoes and went to the cafeteria. Something cool to drink would be good right about now. I picked up two soft drinks and brought them back to the room. Chad was still sleeping quietly. I finished my drink then got back in bed. The rest of the night was peaceful so I slept like a baby.

They released him early that morning but I told him not to return to work for a few days. I took him to his apartment and helped him get settled in to be a bachelor his place was well in order and kept nice. I liked that in a man, it told something about him. The living room was decorated in warm colors, not all loud in zebra or something of the sort that you would expect from a single man. Each room so far was welcoming. I excused myself to go to the bathroom, this would tell the tale. Shocking, it was clean as the rest of the house. No toothpaste stains or hair in the sink. No dirty laundry on the floor, checked the medicine cabinet, inside there was the usual bandages, alcohol, aftershave and two medicine bottles. A part of my wanted to see what he was taking but decided that was going a little too far. I closed it back, washed my hands and went to find him. He was lying across the bed with his eyes closed. I turned to walk away but the sound of his voice asking me to stay brought me to a halt. He asked if I would stay until he went to sleep and of course I said yes. He promised not to try anything if I would lie next to him I did. With one arm placed around me and the other behind his head, he became quiet. His breathing was all of sudden heavy so I knew then he was out.

For a minute I thought we had only been asleep for a few hours but the darkness outside told me different. I tried my best to ease off the bed without awakening him but even the smallest movement woke him. "Sorry Chad, I tried not to wake you. Go back to sleep." Looking at him I could tell he was in pain so I asked him if he was alright. "I have a slight headache and to be honest Sic I am a little hungry." Even if the headache wasn't a good sign the thought of him having an appetite was. Which was good for both he needed food on his stomach before taking anything for pain. I fixed him a sandwich, chips and a soda, placed it beside his bed on the night stand. I think he really was hungry because he at his food in all of 15 minutes. I couldn't help but smile as I reached for his plate. He must have read my mind because he smiled then laughed out loud. I asked if he was ready for his meds and he replied "not if it's going to make me sleepy. I want to enjoy your company while you are here and I can't do that sound asleep." After reading the bottle I told him that it would cause drowsiness but I would be here when he wake. I could tell he was doing his best to fight it off because every time he nodded his body position would change. The medicine finally won the battle and at that very moment he was gone again.

Although he was what seemed to be a neat freak some of his things were out of order so I decided to make wisely of my time and straighten them up a bit. I washed the few dishes we messed up with dinner, did a little dusting in the living room and made my way to the room with the door closed down the hall. I peeped in on Chad as I passed his room and before getting to the door I could hear him snoring. I t wasn't a loud snore but he was snoring. As I turned the doorknob a part of me wasn't sure what could be on the other side of this door but I was about to find out.

The room was dark and had this cold feel to it. There was a small lamp in the far right corner that gave me a little light to see. There were boxes filled with books and picture albums big and small. I knew the pictures had to have been pretty old because the albums looked worn and dusty. On top of the biggest album was a jewelry box that wasn't so old. As a matter of fact I still see this particular style in the stores. Parts of me was saying open it and the other was saying mind your business and get out of this room. The nosey side of me won so I reached for the box and opened it quickly. Inside were lovely pieces of jewelry from a set of chocolate pearls, a ruby ring and a few pairs of diamond earrings of different shapes a gold bracelet and a watch. There were a few more trinkets inside but those weren't that appealing to me. I knew I was pushing it but I tried the ring on just to see if it would fit and it did. Holding my hand up in the mirror I manage to catch a glimpse of Chad standing in the doorway and I dropped the entire box. As it came crashing to the floor throwing all of the jewels out we both reached for items trying to collect them all.

"Chad I am so sorry, this was none of my business and I shouldn't have been in here" I explained while on my knees. "You're right" he said in a strong voice I had only heard once and that was yesterday in the office while on the phone. Something told me I had overstepped my boundaries by entering this room and even more by opening the box. "Chad I promise you if there is anything missing I will replace it with no problem. Once I again I am so sorry for being in here." He wouldn't even look at me. He collected the items and headed to the door. As he reached the door way he turned to look at me with sadness in his eyes he said "some things you can't replace." The sound of his door closing gave me my cue that it was time to go. I gathered my things and left. I didn't say anything before leaving although I wasn't really sure what I would have said.

Walking to my car I couldn't stop thinking about the way he looked as he saw me standing in that room. Whose room was it, if it belonged to anyone and what was with the jewelry? Just like that his expression went from wanting me to wanting me to leave. There was a mystery behind all of this and I wandered if I would ever get to the bottom. Being nosey had hurt his feelings and probably our friendship so I better leave well enough alone. As I approached my car I felt as if I was being watched again. Was this really happening or was it the events of the accident messing with me. I looked around to see if I could spot someone sitting in their car or standing around but there wasn't anyone. Getting into my car I heard another vehicle start then pull off. Checking my rearview mirror I could see lights slowly driving in the opposite direction. Maybe it was my imagination maybe not but I would be careful from this moment on.

Once in my room I took a quick shower and got ready for bed. I listened to the messages I had and made notes of those I would return. It had been a long day that had taken a toll on me. It didn't end the way I would have planned but I guess that's life. I said my prayers found something to watch on television and turned off the lights. Hopefully tomorrow would bring a better day.

The Morning After

The alarm in my room went off exactly 8:30. Felt like I had been sleeping for months. I decided to order room service, get dressed and head to the boutique. Not sure of how Chad was feeling or if he would come in today I would spend some time in the office and see how things were going. I know there is some paper work in there that needs tending to so I would do that. I wanted to call and check on him but after last night that may not be a good idea. If he wants to talk to me he knows where I am and how to get in touch.

As always breakfast was the bomb and the service on time, feeling a little hungry this morning I ordered a waffle, two eggs, bacon and juice. The chef made his waffles from scratch with some secret recipe, trust me they were the best in town. The clock on the wall said 10 o'clock so I knew I better get a move on. Walking pass the front desk the young girl at the counter held out a piece of mail. Told me it was delivered late last night after I got in, they didn't want to disturb me so they held it until morning. There was no return address on it or information indicating where it had come from. The only thing on it was my name inside the envelope was a typed letter with no salutation. For a minute I thought it might have been from Chad but the words in the letter told me different. It read "FUNNY HOW ONE COULD HAVE SO MUCH AND STILL WANT MORE." What did that mean and who could it have come from. Still want more, have so much, I admit I have been blessed and I have worked my ass off for it but I don't have anything anyone else couldn't have. Was this a joke, was it meant for me? I turned and went back to the front desk "where did you get this and are you sure it was meant for me?" She looked at me sort of confused and said "Yes ma'am, a young woman came in here last night very late and said to give this to you Mrs. Sicily Bryant Robinson." She wanted you to receive it then but I told her under orders we are not to disturb the guest that late unless it is an emergency. She told me to make sure you get it this morning then she left." No name was give and none was asked. She described the lady as a middle age, white, long blonde hair and was wearing jeans and a pink shirt. She really didn't give too much information as far as the face was concerned but what she did give didn't ring a bell as far as someone I knew. I guess this is the part of my life where the envy comes out in people and try to scare me but they got the wrong one. I don't scare easy and I love a challenge so bring it on. I threw the letter in my purse strutted to my car and drove off.

The day was a typical business day at the boutique. There were a few customers inside but not too busy for early morning. I really expected more on Saturday but like I said it was early. Stacey was behind the corner doing the usual for her (on the phone). I don't think she was looking for me to come in because soon as she saw me she ended the call fast. It was almost funny to see her stumble but that's what she gets for gossiping so much.

"Hello Mrs. Robinson I didn't know you were coming in today, how are you" she was still looking like a deer caught in the headlights but I will give her credit for trying. "Fine Stacey I'm sure you didn't, I wasn't sure myself until yesterday." I spoke to the customers in the store as I walked passed. Chad was missing in action this morning so I figured I'd better head straight for the office and do some work. As I sat in my chair I couldn't help but notice the flashing light of my answering machine. There were 11 messages and I had a gut feeling they weren't all about business.

The first 8 were pertaining to the store of some sort. Either someone wanted to order an item they were trying to sell something or just wanted to know when they could catch up with me. The last 3 definitely was not business. The ninth message was from a woman looking for Chad. Said she was coming to town and wanted to see him, wanted to know if they could hook up. She also said she was going to pick up lunch and would be waiting for him on Tybee Island and hoped to see him. "Look for the big pink hat." I guess that was her way of making sure he saw her. The next message was from what sounded like the same person at first but the message was for me. Stated she was looking for Mrs. Robinson and we had some unfinished business. She didn't leave a name or number but said she was going to call back later. The last message was also weird, there was no message or anything, all I could hear was the background which was the sound of cars and people passing. I wasn't too sure what that was all about so I wasn't going to worry about it. As for the person looking for me with the unfinished business well they would have to call back. My mind went to the lady with the pink hat. I looked down at my watch to see what time it was. "Almost lunch time" I thought to myself. Maybe I should go to Tybee Island and look for this chick in the pink hat. I was sure Chad hadn't received the message with all the commotion going on so he won't be there. I'm going to check her out myself. I grabbed my things and told Stacey I would return in a couple of hours. This could be interesting.

The Pink Hat

I decided to change from my dress and heels, to something more beach attire, shorts, tank top and flip flops. Of course I kept my shades on just in case this chick knew me and saw me. I guess a lot of people decided to do the beach for lunch today because it was a little bit crowded. I parked somewhat in the middle hoping to Miss Pink Hat before I walked too far. The beach was like a postcard, beautiful day and lots of people. As I sat in the car looking from one end to the other I didn't see anyone wearing a big pink hat. I saw pink scarves and pink caps bouncing around but no pink hats. Guess that means I have to get out and walk. As I unbuckled my seatbelt and opened the door three cars down was a lady in a convertible wearing a big pink hat gathering her things and stepping out of the car, I slowly closed my door and slid down in my seat. I didn't want to move too fast with the fear of her seeing me or blowing my cover.

She reached in the back of her car and retrieved a big basket I assumed it was their lunch. How surprised she will be to find out that he is not coming. I don't know what this heffa is up to or who she is to him but I was going to find out. As soon as she was down the sidewalk and headed for the beach I decided to make my move and get out of the car. Her hat was so big there was no way I was going to lose sight of her. She found a spot just below the pier about a few feet away from the entrance, laid out her lunch for the guest that wasn't coming and sat on the blanket. A group of guys were coming by so I knew if I could get on the far side of them I could make my way to the pier without her even noticing. It worked like a charm. The wind was blowing a little that day so it wasn't too hot. A part of me wanted Chad to show up just to see how they would react to each other but I knew he wasn't coming. Two hours had passed and Miss Thang was still patiently waiting. I don't know if that was a sign of desperation or what but she was still there.

I decided to go ahead and leave. I knew he wasn't coming and nothing was going to happen this time, whether she would be able to get a message to him next time I couldn't say but as for today, nothing was going down. Just was I reached the steps of the pier she gathered her things, threw them in the basket and stomped off in anger, all I could do was stand still as she walked right by me. Had she looked up she would have seen me but full of rage and ready to leave, her eyes were straight ahead. "Whew that was close" I said in a low voice and headed to my car. Before I could unlock my door she had backed out and headed toward town. My private eye instinct told me to follow and see where she was headed so I did my best to catch up. By the time she made it to her third light there was only two cars between us. I couldn't see the expression on her face but the way she was zipping through the cars I could tell she was pissed.

As I followed the chick with the pink hat, I began to notice that we were headed in the area of my store, maybe it was a coincidence but then again maybe not. I was going to give her the benefit of the doubt until we actually come to a stop. We were a few blocks away and if she makes this left turn I will know for sure that's where she was headed. I parked around the block got out and ran to the corner just in time to see her sitting in front of the store the motion of her head told me that she was looking for someone and I knew that someone had to be Chad. After sitting there for what felt like an hour but had only been a few minutes she pulled off mad as ever. "I don't know what Chad has done or who she is to him but she was determined to see him" I thought to myself and I figured I had better tell him.

Once inside the store Jeri couldn't wait to tell me about the woman posted outside. Explained how she sat there looking in from her car with this frown on her face. She also said that she was about to call the police until the lady pulled off. She said a part of her wanted to go ask "what was her problem" but figured that wouldn't be good.

"Has Chad called in yet" I asked before she could say another word. She looked shocked like she wasn't expecting that but she wasn't going to dare say anything out of the way with fear of risking her job. "No ma'am he hasn't called in yet, maybe he will before the day is over. I

sure hope he is ok" she said in a quiet voice. I told her I would go and
check on him if she thought she could handle things by herself for a few
hours. The other clerk had left for the day so I didn't want to put any
pressure on her considering she was only two months new. But I had to
give it to her she had caught on pretty fast. I made sure things were in
order and she had my cell in case she needed me.

The drive to Chad's place was only 30 minutes from the store, a
part of me felt as if I was being followed. I wondered if it was Ms. Pink
Hat but as I looked in the mirror I didn't see a vehicle that resembled
hers. As I got a few blocks away I called him to let him know that I was
coming. Didn't want to surprise him or be surprised. He answered the
phone on the second ring and the sound of his voice told me he was
wide-awake. "Hello this is Chad" he sounded so professional. I told him
that I was in the area and was wondering if I could stop by for a few
minutes. At first there was silence then he said that he didn't mind and
would love to see me. The neighborhood he lived in was a new one and
still had the fresh look. All of the lawns looked manicured and it was
always quiet. I parked my car behind his and walked to the front door.
I couldn't shake the feeling that someone was watching me. As I stood
on the steps I looked around to see if someone was out there watching
but again I saw no one. Maybe it was my conscious playing with me
after watching pink hat today, who knows?

The Visit

Soon as I was inside I felt him looking at me and I couldn't help but look at him. The clean fresh scent coming from his body did something to me. Something about this man always seems to catch me off guard and mesmerize me. I have got to keep control. "Hello Chad, it's good to see you up and moving about. I hope I wasn't interrupting anything. To be honest after you hear what I have to say, you will be more than glad that I stopped." He raised his eyebrow and showed me into the living room. I could hear the sweet sound of Kem coming from his entertainment center. The lights were dimmed and a few candles were lit in each corner. It was almost 5 in the evening so I was wondering what was going on. "Are you sure I'm not interrupting this set up is a little too nice for you to be here alone." Was I being too nosey or what? Either way it goes he will either tell me or he won't. I was hoping he wasn't going to say that he was, I believe I would be crushed. He gave a little smirk as he walked passed me. Into the kitchen I could hear him humming the tune that was playing, nothing else was said so I followed. The smell coming from the kitchen was as breath taking as his scent so I was in heaven.

The kitchen was spotless, other than the items he was using to cook with and the dishes he had set on the table, nothing else was out of place. Looking over his shoulder I noticed two steaks, bake potatoes, salad and garlic bread. A bottle of wine was chilling on the counter with two glasses beside it. I took a deep breath and was about to ask this buster one more time if he was expecting company but before I could answer he turned to face me and gave me that sexy look he always gave that made me weak in the knees. He placed his hands on my shoulders and finally spoke, "Sicily I did this for you, I called the store just a little while ago and Jeri said you'd left. I wanted to surprise you and show you my appreciation for all that you have done." And with that said there was nothing for me to do or say. All I could do was smile and blush. It had been a while since someone had done something so special for me without looking for something in return so it really touched me.

He led me into the dining room and pulled out a chair. I was floating on air at this very moment and didn't want to come down. He returned from the kitchen with a glass of wine in one hand and roses in the other. I noticed each rose was a different color. As he handed me one rose at a time he explained the colors. Pink was for my gentle ways, orange was for the way I carried myself, strong but very lady like and as he handed me the red one I noticed he wasn't saying anything. "Chad are you going to explain the red one or leave me hanging?" I turned to look at him and before I could say anything he leaned into me and placed one of the softest kisses I had experienced directly on my lips. I gave into him as if he was claiming what was his but I knew that couldn't be. I pulled away not really wanting to and after a few moments he spoke.

"Sicily I have tried over and over to stop these feelings I am feeling for you but I can't and I don't think I want too." Was he saying what I thought he was saying? Was he explaining to me in so many words the meaning of the red rose? "I guess what I am trying to say is I'm falling for you, I am starting to love you but I know that cant' be, you are married and I wouldn't want to make your life complicated but lady I can't help myself." All I could say was "damn." He went back into the kitchen and prepared our plates. Everything was picture perfect. It almost made you not want to eat it but I was going to enjoy the meal this handsome man had prepared just for me.

For the first ten minutes we ate in silence. After a few bites here and there I would look up and catch him staring at me. I noticed my hands were a little shaky as I reached for my glass. I was hoping he didn't catch that but I am sure he did. If I'm not mistaken I could have sworn I heard him laugh a little but I paid him no mind. I decided to break the ice and tell him the reason for my visit. "Chad I came over to tell you about this message that was left on the machine for you the other day. I am going to tell you the truth and let you know that in the message she set up a meeting time for you and her and my curiosity got the best of me so I decided to go and see who she was. I hope you aren't mad and I should have told you." I thought he was going to be mad or a little bit pissed but he smiled and started to laugh. "Babe I could never be mad at you for trying to look after me and that's what you were trying to do, did you find out who she was or what she wanted" he really wasn't mad so this made me more comfortable to talk. I told him that I didn't and all I really did was stand back and watch and as she left I followed her to the store. I laughed quietly to myself. He didn't act concerned. I don't know if that was good or bad. Did he have something to hide or was he really not concerned with this lady. Sooner or later I would find out.

He removed the dishes and asked if I wanted to continue in the living room. The music was still playing and over on the table was a miniature waterfall. It was one of the prettiest things I had ever seen. So soothing, relaxing even. As we sat on the couch he placed my legs over his with one swift move. He removed my shoes and began messaging my feet. Thank God for the pedicure the other day I thought to myself. Never catch me slipping on the toes. The treatment he was giving was well welcomed and I hope he knew that. I sat back on the couch and closed my eyes. The long day of private eye and back and forth at the shop had played a toll on me. I must have dozed off because when I opened my eyes my body was covered with a soft blanket and the lights were off. Music was still playing in the background but turned down to a soft whisper and the waterfall was not running. I looked around the room I didn't see Chad so I decided to get up and take a look around. I wanted to call out his name but didn't want to wake him if he was sleep.

The first place I looked was his room. The bed was turned down and the shower was running telling me that's where he was. I sat on the bed waiting to hear the water stop but I ran for a while. Wondering if he was okay I stepped inside the bathroom. Assuming he heard me because he pulled the curtain back and asked me to join him. The shocked look on my face gave the answer. He stepped out all dripping wet steam coming from his body in all the right places. I couldn't move or say a word. The touch of his hands as he removed my clothes piece by piece made me shiver. He took my hand and led me in as I followed. Standing under the hot water he massaged my body with a gel that smelt of lavender, his large hands moved across my skin with a touch soft enough for a baby. The heat from the water was not helping me at all. I was sure that the temperature of my body was way over 100 because I felt faint.

I think he saw it coming because I could feel his body suddenly press against mine. All of this was having an effect on him also because the feel of his erection pressing on my butt told me everything.

As I turned to face this exotic statue his mouth found mine and our lips locked at once. I decided to give in to all he had to offer. My mind couldn't take it and my body needed it. The touch of his tongue as it danced with mine made me welcome him with pleasure. I could still taste the sweetness of the wine on his tongue so I sucked it and held on until I'd had became intoxicated. His kisses lingered from my lips to my face from my face to my neck and from my neck to my breast. He gave them both the attention they yearned for. The water was getting cold but our bodies were good and hot. "Let's take this to the bed" he said raising his head. Dripping wet from head to toe our bodies led a trail from the shower to his bed. I reached for a towel to place over the sheets but he grabbed my hand and told me not to worry. Laying on the bed first he gently pulled me slowly to him, I could feel myself moving in slow motion and I didn't want to stop. He ran his hands all over me touching places that had only been touched by him. Places that Terrence obviously never knew of and places I had forgotten. His touch was a stroke of magic and I was in paradise. We made love with such passion such need for each other's body and searched for what we both longed to find. After long moments of fulfillment we dozed off in each other's arms and slept.

After The Morning After

The sound of his alarm made me jump. I looked over at the clock to see that it was 8:00. Had I actually stayed all night, what would he think but then again this was his idea so I am sure he was pleased. "Morning beautiful, I made you some fresh coffee to start your day." A woman could get use to this. "Chad you are spoiling me and I can't let you keep doing this. Baby I am married or did you forget" his smile turned to a frown and said in a sharp voice, "No sweetie I didn't did you, because the way your body was moving with mine your good ole Terrence was nowhere on your mind either!" I couldn't say a word and he was right. Every word he said was correct. I finished my coffee in bed got dressed and was headed to the door. The feel of his hand on my arm made me stop in my tracks. "I am so sorry I talked to you that way, it was not called for and I don't want any regrets about last night, I don't regret one minute and I hope you don't either." The look in his eyes told me he meant every word. I told him that I didn't and I was where I wanted to be. I held my head down not wanting him to see the tears forming in my eyes. With his hand on my chin he lifted my face and the tears began to flow. Pulling me to him and holding me tight made me know that everything at this moment here in Savannah was going to be okay but was going to take a toll on what was waiting for me in Atlanta. We held each other until the tears stopped and once again I was headed for the door. Being the gentleman he was he walked me to my car.

"What the hell" was all I could say as I noticed the broken glass around my car and missing window from the driver and passenger side? Who could have done this and why. I guess the feeling I got coming here yesterday was right or did they ride by in the middle of the night and find me here? Either way someone was not pleased and I was going to find out why. "Sicily I am so sorry I don't know who could have done this but trust me someone is going to pay" the anger in his voice told me that he cared and that there was strong possibility he didn't know. My mind kept going back to me telling him about the lady in the pink hat. The way he talked as if he didn't know her and wasn't really paying attention to me. Did he have something to hide was this the work of an ex-lover? I really didn't know what to say or how to feel. "I guess I need to call the police and insurance company so that I can get a report." I had to make sure they sent all the information to the store and not the house or there really would be questions asked.

It took all of 9 minutes for the police to show up. The officer came flying around the corner as if we were reporting a murder. "Good morning officers I'm sorry to bother you but someone has broken my windows in my car" one of them introduced himself as Officer Brown, took out his pen and pad and began to ask questions. I told him my name and gave him my insurance card along with my ID. The other guy Officer Scott took pictures of the car and asked Chad a few questions. I couldn't really hear what he was saying so I had no idea what was going on, Officer Brown gave me my items and then out of nowhere said "Mr. and Mrs. Robinson I am very sorry for your troubles hopefully someone saw something and will come forward, if not then there is a big possibility we may not find out who did this." I was about to tell him that Chad was not my husband buy then again would it really matter?

"Now what" I asked Chad. "Let's call a tow truck and have them take the car to the nearest dealership to have it fixed and go by the car rental so you can get something to drive. You will go about your day as if nothing happened and not let this bother you." Wow look at him trying to take control sounding all strong. "Give a man a taste of your goodies and watch him take charge" is what my girl Adriane always said, she was right. I couldn't help but laugh to myself. We waited on the tow truck to come and then went to the rental. I had a really bad feeling about the whole situation. Something wasn't right and I was beginning to think it had something to do with this good looking man sitting next to me. What were you not telling me Chad, are you hiding something? Whatever it is I hope it's not going to be something really bad. My gut was telling me pink hat had something to do with it but if I find out this chick broke my windows, she will be wearing a black hat and dressed casket sharp.

I picked a black Maxima, to drive the next few days the dealership told me my car would be ready the next day but I was going to put her in Chad's garage until I was headed back home. Chad went ahead of me to the store. I guess the only thing he had on his mind now was getting back to work but my mind was full of drama. The store was pretty packed for early evening but I was pleased. Jeri was helping a few customers and Chad was in the back doing paper work. As the crowd soon settled Jeri came in the back and asked if she could speak to me for a minute. "We had a customer come in today and linger in the store for a while today she didn't buy anything, just stayed in the store she wasn't a usual customer but she did look familiar to me, then it hit me she was the lady that sat outside in the car the other day. Just figured you wanted to know." I told her thank you for the information and then decided to go look at the tape. Although I had never seen her face I knew right off the bat that this was Ms. Pink Hat. All I need now was for her to turn and face the camera so I can get a good look. After a few minutes of watching I was beginning to think she was never going to look up then as she was leaving Jeri said something to her and she looked up. Now finally I had a face to go along with all this mystery.

I called Chad in and told him we needed to look at the security tape, I didn't tell him why. I wanted to see the look on his face. We sat there for a few minutes then just as she looked up at Jeri I turned to him, the look on his face was priceless. He knew who she was and was going to tell me here and now. I walked to the front and told Jeri we would be in a meeting if she needed anything to buzz the office phone. When I returned I found Chad pacing the floor with his face in his hands. Hearing the door close and lock caused him to look at me. "Who is she Chad and don't you are lie!"

All he could do was shake his head, then said "she is my ex-wife, I am so sorry Sicily. I should've been honest with you from the beginning but that's a part of my life that I have put behind me and until now it has stayed there for 5 years. I haven't seen or heard from Michelle in all this time so I have no idea what she wants now. I promise you whatever this is it won't interfere with my job or this. Trust me."

I can't even lie the word ex and wife hit my stomach like a brick. Was he one of those brothers with a past that with a lot of drama? One thing I know for sure is he is very good at what he does for all that stand for and she was not going to mess that up. If she thought she was going to come here and start trouble she got another thing coming. I made no comment to what he said just held on to the last words, trust me and that's what I was going to do til he showed me different.

Terrence's Call

As I sat in my room that night trying to piece together all that had happened I couldn't help but wonder what would happen next. I had a face for her and now there was a name, was she the one that broke the window in my car, did she know about the other night and had been watching me all this time? I had questions but no answers. At that very moment the phone rang, I looked at my caller id and saw that it was Terrence. Hadn't heard from him in two days which wasn't like him and now all of a sudden he wants to call at this hour. "Hello Terrence, I was beginning to think you had forgotten about me. How are things going on that end and how are the boys?" He told me everything was fine, he had gotten the contract in South Carolina and that the boys were great. He asked if I had plans on coming home soon and about the store. That was shocking because its rare that he would even ask about the store, he would usually throw it in as how are things or something of the sort but not the store. What really got me was when he asked about Chad. "How is Mr. Jackson doing, is he performing to your status?" A part of me felt like he was trying to be funny as if he really wasn't concerned but what the hell. After having a day like today I was not going to argue with him. "He is doing fine, hitting home runs at what he does best. Hiring him was a good decision" I said being just as smart as he was. "Im sure" was all he said then changed the subject.

"So Mrs. Robinson when are you coming home, you do know that you are married with three kids and a business here in town also" he said with such bass in his voice. Was he serious about his attitude? He knows that has never fazed me and wasn't about too. I told him how could I forget when I am there half of the time he wasn't and when he is its always business and short talk with him so I am very aware of what's waiting for me at home. "Yes Mr. Robinson I will be home Saturday evening." We said our I love you and goodbyes then hung up the phone. With two days left I would have to do a lot of snooping, investigating and whatever else I had to do to get some answers before heading home. I was not going back with a lot of unanswered questions hanging over my head. First thing in the morning I was going to check on my car then head to my main priority, my Savannah store, but for now I am going to call Adriane, my best bud and fill her in. I am sure she will have some questions, answers and threats knowing her.

She answered the phone after the second ring. "Heffa it is 2 in the morning, you better be in the hospital, in jail or on the side of road. If it's the last one then I know this is a misdial for the auto shop." Even in the wee hours of the morning she was full of jokes, I will call them, that's why I loved her so much. "Sorry about this friend but so much has gone on that I had to call you before turning in." I could hear her sitting up in bed so I decided to continue. I told her about the girl in the store, Ms. Michelle and how she was Chad's exwife and also about my car. She cleared her throat and in one puff gave me "So I guess we have gone from being a boutique owner to private eye and does all of your male employees at the other stores get these benefits in their package and more importantly do you need me to come down there and kick some ass cause I am willing to bet she is the one that messed with your car." Like I said earlier questions, answers and threats all in one breathe.

We talked on the phone for about an hour then I knew I had to let her get some rest and I was in need of some also. I promised to call her tomorrow once I got settled for the day and update her on everything and also to call her if I needed her before getting home. I took a shower, laid my clothes out for the next day and jumped in the bed. I was good and tired now and was going to sleep peacefully.

Just Another Day

I picked up some coffee and bagels for the employees at the store on my way in at this little bistro on the water front. The store was quiet Jeri had the day off so I had the pleasure of working with Amanda and Fayla. Chad was pulling up as I walked in so I was wondering what his attitude would be like. Amanda and Fayla were from the Manhattan store, a lot of our new fashions came from up there so once a month they would fly down with some new things and get a feel of the customers down here before we actually brought the new line to the south. Fashion was funny that way some styles never made it here and vice versa.

"Good morning Mrs. Robinson" the ladies said together as if it was rehearsed. I told them good morning and that there was coffee and bagels in the kitchen. Their visits were never more than a few days and I really enjoyed them. They came, did their thing and left. If the items were a hit they would return in a few weeks, set up new displays and be on their way back once more. I can honestly say I was blessed with a good group of employees and as for the little mess going on surrounding Chad, drama was something we didn't have and they never brought.

"Hello ladies" he said coming in carrying a platter of fruit he picked up from the store down the road. I could tell by their signature wrapping. He looked at me and the bags I was holding and ended with "I guess great minds think alike". He turned to walk to the kitchen and I followed. Placing our items on the table he looked at me, gave me a wink and headed to the office. I really didn't know what to say to him or if I wanted to say anything at all. I closed the door behind me got down to work and never looked his way. I guess he could sense the little tension in the room cause without saying anything he walked out. Time must have crept up on me, looking at the clock two and half hours had past just like that. I closed the folders, gave my body a good stretch then moved to the front of the store. It was almost lunchtime so I knew the customers would be coming soon. The lunch crowd always came through for us and in a good number. They were the ones getting ready to hit the street when their work shift was over or they made a mess of their attire during lunch and needed to grab a clean blouse or skirt. No matter what the reason was for their visit we welcomed them all with open arms and working registers. Haha.

Fayla was taking care of two girls that were interested in the samples she had brought and Amanda and Chad were working on a display in the window. Everyone was doing their thing, the sun was shining bright and laughter was in the air. What could go wrong? Before I could get that thought out of my mind I noticed Chad straighten his stand and drop the piece of clothing in his hand. My eyes followed him to the lady coming in the door, I be damned if it wasn't Michelle. I think Amanda could sense the tension in the air because she stopped what she was doing and headed to greet our customer. "Hello, welcome to Bella Signora (it was Italian for Lovely lady), is there anything I can help you with today?" Before Amanda could finish her sentence Michelle but her off and said "No thank you, I didn't come here to shop I came to speak to my husband, my bad ex-husband. Hello Chad."

He was as speechless as I was. Was this chick trying to make herself known and I know she wasn't about to start some mess in here. Fayla finished checking the two ladies out at the counter and walked them to the door. The ladies walked between Chad and Michelle but they never lost eye contact. "Hello my name is Sicily and you are?" I said holding out my hand to shake hers and hopefully break some of this tension. She turned to look at me but not with pleasure, one of those how dare you looks but she knew not to say anything out of line. "My name is Michelle Jackson as I said earlier I am his ex-wife." No this heffa didn't have attitude. "As I said earlier, in my I don't give a damn voice, my name is Sicily Bryant Robinson and this is my store!" She must have taken the hint because she then asked Chad if there was somewhere they could talk. I told him to feel free to use the office or step outside for a few minutes. He headed in the direction of the office with her in tow. Lord what I would give to be a fly on the wall.

I walked over to the counter trying to find something to do. Fayla and Amanda both came over to see if what was going on. I didn't want to give too much detail and wasn't going to give any details about us. "Sicily you know if you hit the blue button on the alarm pad you can hear whatever is going on in the other rooms but they cant hear you. It's a new protection thing that came with all the systems you when you upgraded the stores." Amanda was always on top of things and she must have been reading my mind because I was 5 seconds from standing in the hall way. "Sicily if he really wanted to you know what they were saying he would have told her to speak to him here." Damn, always the reasonable one in the bunch and Fayla was right. Amanda and I both looked at her at the same time then walked over to the keypad.

Although they said they wouldn't be able to hear me I put my finger to my lips telling them to be quiet then pressed the button.

"Michelle what the hell are you doing here, how did you know where I was and when the hell are you leaving?" Chad had a lot of anger in his voice and to be honest I was glad to hear him talking to her in such a manner. All I wanted was answers and for her to leave.

"Chad I can't believe you are talking to me like this. You use to love me and we share a past." Michelle sounded like one of those whining chicks that every black woman hated. I guess the next thing for her to do was to start begging. "Please talk to me Chad and don't be angry. After our divorce you left me without a trace or even a decent goodbye. I didn't know where you were or where to send your mail." She sounded sad.

"So you came to give me my mail. Thank you and goodbye." I had never heard him talk to anyone like that. The room was quiet and we were wondering what was going on then he spoke. "I figured the divorce papers was a sign it was over and there was nothing else to say. I didn't tell you where I was going or how to get in touch with me because I didn't ever want to hear from your trifling ass again. So there you have it in a nut shell, will you please leave." At that moment we heard the door open and heavy footsteps coming in our direction. I pressed the off button and acted like I was straightening the clothes on the rack beside me. I didn't know which direction the girls had gotten off too and wasn't about to look for them. Other customers were coming in the door so I was really praying this wasn't about to get ugly.

She called his name out loud one last time and told him he couldn't walk away from her like this. I stepping in front of her and said with a straight face that she was in a place of business and this will have to end here for now. That there wasn't going to be a scene in my store and I wasn't asking her to leave but telling her ass to go. Michelle told him that it wasn't over and he would see her again. "Not here I hope" I said as she walked out. Chad asked if he could see me in the back, I knew he wanted to explain and I wanted to hear it. Before heading to my office I turned to the ladies and told them to stay away from the keypad, smiled and left.

Once in the back he pulled me to him and held me tight. I didn't know what to do or say so I just held on to him. His breathing was heavy and I could feel his heartbeat. He kissed me on my neck and whispered he was sorry. I knew I shouldn't be feeling like this but being in his arms as close as we were always did something to me. I whispered back that it was okay and it will work itself out. He told me that he wanted to explain but not here. We made plans to meet later but this time he would come to me. The rest of the evening went well. I figured I would leave first because I didn't want anything looking suspicious to the girls. I stopped at the corner store to pick up a few things. Didn't want room service because they could be very nosey also, I grabbed a bottle of Verdi and a few deli sandwiches. Passing by the produce section I couldn't help but notice the sweet smell coming from the strawberries so I grabbed some of them. Looking at the items in my buggy you would think I had some romantic plans but that wasn't it at all. It was what I usually had when I wanted to relax with something light.

Back at my room the light was blinking on the phone indicating there was a message. I decided to take a shower and get dressed before Chad arrived. Nine times out of ten it was Adriane calling. She was very impatient and probably was wondering what was going on. I turned on the shower and would call when I got out. Before I could dry off good and pull my hair back in a ponytail there was a knock at the door. Chad was always on time so I knew it had to be him. I grabbed my terry cloth robe and ran to the door. Starring at him through the peep hole I could help but wonder what secrets this man held. More importantly would we get to hold each other one more time? He entered with a bouquet of flowers and a bottle of wine. Nothing like a man to come bearing gifts, the wine was one of my favorites and there were six roses, two pink, two orange and two red. I remembered what he said the first time he gave those colors and figured things were a little stronger because they were doubled. "Chad you didn't have to do that, you came here to talk and get some things off your mind' I was trying to sound sincere but I really enjoying his thoughtfulness. I had received more gifts and attention from him in the past few months than I had from Terrence in the past few years. He followed me into the sitting room and out to the patio. I told him since it was such a beautiful night I figured we could sit out. All of the items I had purchased earlier were laid out nicely on the table. "Let me get dressed and I will be right back." Before I could walk away good he grabbed my hand and pulled me to him. With one move his lips were on mine and the sash on my robe was undone. The feel of his hands caressing my still damp body was one I didn't want to end. If this was his way of asking for forgiveness then it was done.

His hands slowly drifted to my butt and squeezed it tight. Rubbing against each other must have gotten to him because I could feel his erection through his pants. I unbuckled the leather belt that held it all together jeans fitted him like they were tailor made. a pair of silk blue boxers was the only thing between us so they had to go. He sat down in the chair and gently pulled me onto his lap. Our bodies fit like a glove and with the drama that had been going on around us the past few days it was what we needed and wanted. After both of our bodies were satisfied and relaxed I decided to get dressed for real this time so we could talk. While in the room there was a knock on the door. I figured around this time of night it had to be room service. "Chad get that please" I yelled from inside. Once dressed I headed for the patio announcing my entrance "baby was that room service" I asked again. Looking at him I saw the same look he had in the store when he saw Michelle, on his face right now. "No baby it's not" came from a voice that sounded a lot like Terrence. I turned in the direction of Chad's stare only to find Terrence there full of rage.

They Meet

I froze in my tracks. Standing there trying to find my voice. Looking back and forth from Chad to Terrence I was speechless but Terrence wasn't. "Now I see why my wife can't bring her ass home, brotha you must be putting it down on her good. I see you're a little younger than us both so I assume you banging the hell out of her." I couldn't believe he was saying that. I had never heard him talk like that. "Terrence sweetie it's not like that, we were discussing business." Now I was sounding like the begging sistah. "Oh really and since when did wine and strawberries become part of the business. I see my man here came prepared with roses. Is that all it takes to hump my wife? Damn I see I spent too much money back in the day." Was Terrence calling me cheap, was he calling me a hoe? Whatever he was trying to say must have pissed Chad off cause with one blow he knocked the hell out of Terrence and to the floor he went. "Chad no, what are you doing" I couldn't believe what was going on, where did Terrence come from and why at this hour? When we last talked I explained I would be home Saturday and would see him then.

After shaking off Chad's punch and wiping his eye he turned to me and said "I see my mystery call was right, there is something going on between you and your do boy. Either you ask him to leave and we settle this or I leave and it's over." With tears in my eyes I turned to Chad and asked him to leave. Terrence went in the bathroom to clean up as I walked him to the door. I whispered to him I would talk to him later but he pushed me away and left.

"Sicily I don't know what is going on between you and him but for the past few days I've been getting weird phone calls and messages left on my machine about my wife and her help. I don't know who it is calling but from the looks of things she was right so as I asked earlier, what the hell is going on?" I really didn't know what to say or where to begin but it wasn't all going to be the truth. "Chad and I are just friends, he is going through some things right now and I was trying to help him by talking to him away from work. His ex-wife showed up at the store today and tried to cause a scene but we stopped her before she could get started" I was talking so fast I had to catch my breath. I hope he believed what I was saying and that it would calm him down because I didn't want to tell anything else. He sat down on the bed still holding his eye. This had been a hell of a week and I would do whatever I needed to changed it all if I could but we were too far gone and I had to roll with the punches. "Sicily is that why you are driving a rental car, did she or he do something to your car?" How did he know all of that? I was shocked and didn't dare to answer. I went on and on about Chad and what was going on with him. There was no way in the world showing up tonight was a coincidence and who was calling him anyway? How much did he know? I didn't want to get to close so I sat in the chair across from him and never said a word. Were we going to be able to fix it, did I want to fix it?

What felt like hours had passed before Terrence looked at me. Still without saying a word he got up and walked out. That was it, we were through. I waited a few minutes to see if he was coming back but he never did. I ran to the door praying he was in the hallway but he wasn't. How did I let this happen? Things weren't suppose to turn out this way. Did I get caught up between love, happiness and infatuation? I am too old for this. I thought I had my shit together but I guess I was wrong. Is he coming back or did he go home to pack my things? I wasn't sure what was going to happen but nevertheless it was facing me now.

I almost didn't hear my phone ringing on the table and wasn't sure if I had any missed calls but I decided to check it anyway. "Hello this is Sicily" it took a minute for the person to respond then I heard "Baby don't say a word just walk over to the balcony and look across the street." It was Chad of all people. A part of me was hoping it would be Terrence. Several hours had passed and he hadn't called or returned. When I called his phone it went straight to voicemail so I stopped trying. As I looked across the street I could see Chad standing out in the open with more flowers in his hand. "Sicily I am so sorry, I never meant for you to get caught up like this. I guess I was focusing more on my needs and wants, not yours and I was wrong. I saw your husband leave a while ago and wondered if he was going to return. After several hours I decided to call." He always had a way with words and knew exactly what to say. I guess that's why I loved him, I said to myself. Did I just say what I thought I said? I love Chad Jackson.

It slipped out so fast maybe I wasn't thinking right. The night had been long and confusing and everything else you could think of. I was brought back to life by the sound of Chad's voice calling me. "Yes Chad I am still here. I don't know where Terrence went and he hasn't called. Maybe that's my cue to gather my things and return home." The phone went silent. The only thing could be heard was his breathing. Was he upset or did he understand? "Sic I can't tell you what to do and I want you to be happy. A big part of me was hoping I could be the one that makes you happy but you need to decide that. I won't try to keep you here. I have some business I need to bring to an end and someone I need to get out of my life for good. Nothing will change as far as the shop. If you will still have me as your assistant I would love to keep my job." The thought of the shop and his employment there never crossed my mind. Along with everything else he was a good worker, nothing could change that and I would be a fool to let him go. "Chad the job is till yours and I trust you will continue to go good work as you have in the past. Keep my updated on things and still call me if you need me but I must head back to Atlanta." Looking down across the street I watch him place the flowers on the curb and quietly whisper "I love you." He placed the phone on the receiver and disappeared into the night.

As I checked out of the hotel and headed to my car, the feel of someone watching me was lingering again. Was it Chad, Terrence or Michelle? Whoever it was I couldn't worry about that now. I had bigger fish to fry back home and it wasn't going to be easy.

Drama At Home

The drive home was a very tense drive. I didn't know what to expect once I got there. Did Terrence come home pissed enough to throw me out, did he tell my boys what had happened or did he even come home at all. As I pulled in the driveway Clifford, Terrell and two other friends were outside shooting hoops. They met me as I got out of the car, all loving and caring as usual so I'm thinking he didn't say a word to them.

"Hey mom how was Savannah and the shop holding up, is old dude doing his thang" Clifford said trying to sound all cool. I told him he was doing a great job and Savannah was still beautiful. "Are you tired" Terrell said as he leaned over and kissed my cheek. "A little bit but I am good. Take my things to my room please while I sit in the den and go over the mail. Where is your father" I asked trying to sound all calm. Clifford told me he wasn't sure. Terrence left yesterday morning so Clifford really couldn't say. I tried to call his cell once I finished the mail and still no answer. I called his friend Bernard who usually keeps up with him but for the first time he had no idea, unless he was lying for him. All I know is tomorrow was a work day and the Terrence I know wouldn't miss that unless it was an emergency.

I didn't feel like cooking so I let the boys order in for everyone, even for Terrence who was a no show. We decided to watch a move while we at. Terrell chose a comedy which was a good choice considering the circumstance. Once the movie was over the kitchen was clean and baths were taken I went to the their room as I usually do just to see if there was something on their minds. Clifford's room was neat and in order. Every once in a while his shoes would be in the floor but other than that it was clean. "Sweetie how are things going" I asked as he was turning his linen back. He told me he was fine, school was good, his girlfriend was good and home was good. What more could I ask for. "How are things for you" he hit me in return and I wasn't expecting it. This would be one of the times I would lie to my son "Everything is good Cliff, just staying busy, holidays are coming up and new things coming in so I'm excited." We talked a little more about school and I listened as he dropped hints about what he wanted for Christmas then we called it a night. My children were never picky, never asked for anything over the top and always thankful for everything they got so in my eyes we were blessed. As long as they stayed out of trouble, got their work done in school and at home I had no problems. I pulled the cover over his shoulders, kissed him on the forehead and switched the light off beside his bed. As I turned to walk out I heard him tell me he loved me and was glad I was home. I knew Terrell wouldn't be asleep, he would be in bed but wide awake for hours. I heard music playing as I approached his door so I knew he was up. "What's up mom" he was always laid back. "Nothing Terrell just wanted to tuck you guys in, I have really missed you. Also I wanted to get a feel of what you wanted for Christmas this year, I asked Clifford and we all know he wants a new car." We talked about the same things as I did with Clifford, school, girls and relationships. Seemed like he had it all together, he never let anything bother him much as I was proud of that. I kissed his cheek turned off the light, told him I loved him and closed the door.

Walking to my room I couldn't help but feel a sense of loneliness which had become a lot here lately, or should I say when I was away from Chad. I was hoping by now Terrence would've been home or at least coming in the driveway but still nothing. I did the only thing I could do, I called Adriane. The phone rang three times before she answered "What's up Sic, haven't heard from you in a minute. I usually get a call every day, I was getting worried." She was right and I had, but the past few days had been out of control still that was no excuse. I started from two days ago and brought her up to present. At first she was quiet then she came out with "Damn it Sicily you have got to be kidding me, are you okay and what are you going to do now." To be honest I hadn't really thought of that. I guess you could say I was playing it by ear, making each decision as it approached me. I never thought what it Terrence didn't come home or suppose he wanted a divorce and suppose his agenda was to tell the boys and make them hate me. Then again my boys love me so that's something I wouldn't have to worry about. The would be mad of course but hate me, no. I finished my call with Adriane, checked my messages and decided to get some rest. Who knows what tomorrow may bring.

I woke up the next morning to the smell of pancakes and bacon. Knowing how my boys drag early in the morning I couldn't believe they had gotten up and prepared breakfast. I showered and dressed quickly, didn't want to miss them before they headed out the door. But to my surprise as I reached the kitchen it was Terrence that had prepared breakfast for us. He was humming a familiar tune that I couldn't quite name, smiling all bright, even at me. "Hello my lovely wife, how did you sleep" was this joker on drugs, was he planning to kill me with this food, could there be poison in here? A million things ran through my head as I watched him act as if nothing had happened. The boys came running in the kitchen all ready to dive in and thanking their dad at the same time. Terrence had fixed my plate as well as his own. Two pancakes, bacon and eggs. I wasn't feeling his show right now and was not going to trust him after what happened the other day. Soon as he turned his back to get the juice I switched our plates not aware that Clifford saw me until he said "mom what are you doing?" all I could say was "your dads looked more fluffy", smiled and said grace. The boys ate in a hurry then rushed off to school. They didn't play that being late or missing a day unless they had too and I loved them for it. Terrence asked if I had a big day planned and if I wanted to meet for lunch at our usual spot, we hadn't done that in months so I didn't know what to think. I told him yes and that I would call him around eleven to make sure he was still available. "Of course I will anything for my lady" he said as he drank the last of his juice getting up from the table. Was this bastard playing mind games with me? Did he really think he was going to run me crazy or something? If he did he had another thing coming. Mama didn't raise no fool, you can bet your bottom dollar on that shit. He wanted to play then damnit lets play. I gave him a hug and a kiss and said thank you for a wonderful breakfast, grabbed my things then was out the door. As soon as I was out the driveway and down the road I called Adriane and told her of his little show. "Girl there is no way in hell I would have eaten anything he cooked. You did the right thing by switching plates. His ass is up to something so you better stay on your toes." As hard as she sound she was definitely right.

Later that morning I called him a little after eleven, he answered on the first ring which was not like him at all. "Hey babe, how is your day going are you ready to meet for lunch" he was all excited and full of spunk like he had an audience, he said he could swing by an pick me up from the shop that way I would have to fight the traffic. I knew then something was up because he never offered to do that before. He was over in Austell and I was in Stone Mountain so he would have a nice drive not to mention the restaurant was in the middle of them both. I told him that would be nice and I'd be waiting with bells on, more like a barbell in my purse if he tried anything fishy I was going to clock his ass good.

He was on time all smiles and opening doors. As we drove downtown I paid attention to the song he was playing on the cd player. It was Love Calls by Kem. Chad always had it playing in his car and in the office. I can never remember Terrence ever listening to Kem before. Was this a new thing he had picked up? The restaurant was not packed but had just enough people in there to make it a nice crowd. We sat at our usual table, ordered our usual lunches and at in silence. Every once in a while I would look up and notice Terrence watching me. What was he thinking? Was it something evil or was he changing? Considering the fact he had been getting phone calls about his wife and had caught Chad in my hotel room I am going to go with evil for 200 Alex. Lol. We finished our meals, paid the tab then headed to the car. I wasn't going to say anything if he wasn't, the ride back to the shop was as quiet as the one going to lunch. Once we were in front of the boutique he jumped out to open my door and walked me inside. "I'll see you this evening sweetie, I promise I won't be late." Then he kissed my forehead and headed back to his side of town. This was now getting to me and I wasn't sure what was going to be the outcome but I was going to keep my eyes open and on him. This was not what I had expected.

I finished all of my work in the office for the day. Made my weekly calls to the other stores as usual on Mondays and decided to go home. Lasagna was going to be on the menu tonight and not sure of what was at the house I knew I had to stop by the grocery store. I had used the same grocer for the past six years and had no intention of changing. Their meat, produce and bread were always fresh not to mention the dairy items were never out of date. Everyone from the cashiers, bagboys and management always had a smile on their face. It gave you a good feeling to be in their store. I decided to do a garden salad and garlic bread with the lasagna, wine for Terrence and I and soda for the boys. The lines were moving pretty swift so the wait wasn't long. On the drive home I decided to listen to the cd Chad made for me before I left Savanna on a past visit. He said the songs on here made him think of me and the times we shared and he found himself listening to them often. He placed the song Love Calls by Kem on there twice. It was his favorite of all the songs on there and said it gave a message. After hearing the song the first time I fell in love with it and didn't mind the fact that it was on there twice. Matter of fact hearing it made me go out and purchase his entire cd. The thought of the song took me back on the drive with Terrence, not saying he doesn't like nice music but this wouldn't be one of the songs I could actually say he'd pick. Had he heard me play it, I don't think so because I have always kept the cd in my car and I never let anyone borrow them. For some reason this song and Terrence didn't connect and it was really bothering me.

Turning into the driveway I noticed the house looked quiet as if no one was there. If it wasn't for the car in the garage I would have thought exactly that. Then it hit me as to what time it was, usually around this time of day the boys are either taking a nap or studying. As I made my way into the kitchen with the bags all I could hear was the television playing in the den. Peeping inside both boys were stretched out on the floor fast asleep. I hadn't heard from Randall in a while so I decided to give him a call. "Hi mom, what's up, how's my favorite girl doing" I really did miss him and was so happy to hear his voice. "I'm doing good son how are you" he told me all was well and that his grades were good. I never had a feeling they would be anything less because even in high school Randall was a great student.

We talked a little while longer discussing his plans for the holidays. He said I had no worries that he was coming home for a week and really was looking forward to it. After my talk with him I went upstairs to change clothes so that I could prepare dinner. As usual Terrence left his clothes on the floor in the bathroom so I decided to pick them up and place them in the hamper. Reaching to pick the shirt up I noticed a receipt sticking out of the pocket so I figured I'd better take a peak just in case it was important. It was a gas receipt from a store whose name was familiar. I thought and thought and it finally hit me, this store was in Savannah. I looked at the date and saw that it was around the time

Chad had his accident. As I recalled it was also the time Terrence was supposed to be in the Carolina's checking on a project. Could I have been wrong did I have the dates mixed up? I doubt that but there was only one way to find out. I pulled my checkbook out and went through all of the checks that were written that month. I remember clearly writing a check for some items I took to the hospital for Chad. The date on the duplicate was the day after the date on the receipt. That couldn't be! Was he lying the entire time and was he hiding something? When I told him of the accident he really didn't seem concerned although he was not a fan of Chads from the beginning. I held on to the piece of paper and decided I would say anything to him but would definitely be calling my girl before the night was over. I wasn't sure what Terrence was up to but I was going to find out. I left the clothes on the floor and put the receipt in my purse.

As I made it back downstairs to the kitchen I could hear his truck pulling in the yard. Could be keep a straight face and lie through his teeth, hell yes. This was Terrence I was talking about so I knew this was going to be good. "Hi sweetie how was your day" I asked in a Carol Brady type manner. He told me that it was fine and he was glad to be home. Yeah I am sure he was so I asked another question. "Have you heard anything else from the contract in Carolina"? He turned and looked at me with a bewildered kind of you look, he was silent for a few seconds then answered "they decided to put things on hold for a bit, maybe it will pick up for them soon." He turned back around and walked off. I knew then he was lying. I was going to get to the bottom of this if it was the last thing I did.

The dinner table was quiet, no one said a word. It felt a little funny knowing that the atmosphere was from me and Terrence so I decided to break the ice. "Terrence there is an event coming up soon in Savannah and I was hoping we could attend. That's if you can take some time off" who was I kidding, this guy was not going to miss work and to go to Savannah was really out of the question. That would be putting him a little too close for comfort. He put his fork down, took a drink from his glass and to my surprise looked at me and said "sure". I almost choked. I couldn't believe it. Now I know something is up but what? The Terrence I know wouldn't take off when he had walking pneumonia but now he was willing to take off for one of my events. This was going to be good.

I cleared the table when our meal was finished, cleaned the kitchen, kissed my boys good night then decided to turn in early. A nice soak in the tub was what these bones needed and was going to get. Reaching the top of the stairs I could hear Terrence on a deep conversation. I heard the words Savannah and hurt. Who was he talking to and what were they talking about? I guess this was a hint for me to be on my p's and q's while we were down there. Mr. Robinson had something up his sleeve and from the looks of things he wasn't working alone.

By the time I showered and got dressed for bed Terrence was already sleep. I don't know if that was good or bad. Usually he would stay awake and wait for me to get in bed before going to sleep but I guess some things were changing. I didn't ponder on the matter long, decided I had dealt with a long day and a good night rest would be just what I needed so I turned off the lights, said my prayers and closed my eyes.

The next morning was just as quiet as dinner was the night before. The boys were up and out by the time I made it to the kitchen. Terrence, to my surprise, had prepared a little but nourishing breakfast, bagels, fruit and coffee. What was this guy up to? He wasn't going to be able to keep this up so eventually I would find out. We both said good morning and exchanged blank looks and kisses. After breakfast I gathered my things and told him I would call him later, we usually discussed lunch but not today, goodbyes were given and we were off in different directions.

I realized I hadn't spoken to Chad since returning home so I decided to give him a call. He picked up on the first ring so it caught me off guard. "Hello Sicily, I wanted to call you but decided it might be best if I waited on you to call me, how are you" he said so much so fast I dint know where to start. Could that have been a sign that I was missed? Of course this was a thought I kept to myself.

"Hello Chad, I hope everything is going ok with you and the store, have you followed up with the doctor like you promised?" I was sounding more like a mother. He told me that all was good and the store was going great, we talked about the even the city was bringing to Savannah within the next week. I told him that Terrence and I would be attending. Maybe it was me but it sure did sound as if his entire mood changed. I didn't let him know that I was aware of it as we finished the conversation. He did offer to make arrangements for our stay but I told him I would handle it. I remember feeling distant as we ended our call.

So much had happened over the past few months but I knew there was some closeness and lots of feelings shared between us. As I drove down the highway I decided to play the cd he made for me a while back. It always seem to put me in a good mood and at this point I was hoping it still did.

As I arrived at my office the thought of calling Chad back was all over me. Sure there was something he needed and wanted to say, did he get upset at the thought of Terrence coming with me? All of these things I needed to know and was going to find out as soon as I sat behind my desk. Listening to the messages on my machine I couldn't help but notice the 4 calls that sounded like someone was holding the phone and breathing heavily. Was it Chad's ex trying to scare me? If it was then she better try again cause I don't scare that easily. To my surprise Chad had left two messages since the other day. I couldn't believe he hadn't called my cell phone. He usually would call that phone before calling anywhere else. I decided I really needed to call Mr. Jackson to see just what was on his mind.

The phone rang three times then went to voicemail. "Chad this is Sicily, I really feel we need to talk whenever you get a chance, call me back and this time call my cell. Hope to hear from you soon." I kept the message short, sweet and to the point. The rest of the morning flew by and before I knew it lunch time had arrived. I decided to call Adriane and have her meet me at the spot.

We sat at our table, ordering the usual and catching up. I told her everything that had been going on, even told her what Terrence had been up too and she thought the thing I had been thinking but afraid to admit. There was a possibility he was behind all the things that had been happening to me and Chad, we just couldn't prove it. She told me that the trip to Savannah would probably bring some things to light but just wasn't sure how or when. The only other thing we couldn't put our finger on was who the other person was on the end of the phone he was talking to the other night. Like Adriane said all this mess going to come out, just hope it don't get ugly.

Three Is A Crowd

Although the big event in good old Savannah was this coming Saturday we decided to come down early Friday morning. This would give us the opportunity to do some shopping, visit the beach and for me to check on the store. I decided to stay at the Inn on the beach, wouldn't dare think of staying at the same place Terrence caught me and Chad. Talk about a hellafied weekend. I can just imagine Terrence "Is this the same bed, did you both shower here, I'm sure you have plenty of memories Sicily." So I decided to play it smart and pick an entirely different area.

The rooms weren't as big as the ones I was use to but they were comfortable and very clean. The service downstairs had been good so there was no reason to complain, at least for now. It was almost noon so we decided to go for lunch and then do some shopping along the pier. Karen's was the spot Terrence chose. Just walking through the door made me think of the last night I was there with Chad. To add fuel to the fire we sat at the exact same table. Was this a sign of how my weekend was going to go? As we sat and looked over the menu the smooth groove of Ledisi singing Alright played and eased the tension of the moment for me. I think that was my sign that things were going to be just fine. As usual Terrence was his in charge self "Sicily why don't you let me order the food and you order the drinks?" I didn't feel like arguing and what would have been the use, this was nothing new so I was use to it. So my dear husband ordered the food and I ordered the wine and we were both content, or so I thought. When the waiter brought the food to my surprise it was the same waiter that had served Chad and I. "Lord these signs are confusing me" I thought to myself. So I just decided to go with the flow and not worry.

As he placed our plates in front of us I couldn't help but notice him watching me so I looked up at him. As soon as our eyes met he looked at me then at Terrence then back at me. Was he trying to tell me that he remembered me being there with someone else? What was his nosey ass implying? One thing for sure he had better serve the food and let well enough alone. I was not in the mood for Terrence's shit or his so he better be careful. We ate our food in peace, no smart remarks or sharp looks just peace and trust me I really needed that. Deciding against desserts we paid the check, left a tip better than I had planned and headed for the pier. It was almost after 3 and I was getting tired. Terrence had mentioned several times that he had left his tie at home that went with the suit he brought so we stopped in one of the men stores to get him another one.

Of course he wanted everyone else opinion except for mine and as tired as I was I could really care less. As he and the sales lady talked about the ties for what felt like hours I decided to walk to the other side of the store and look at the different suits that were on display. I found myself trying to picture Chad in the black one. All sharp and clean, fit to a t, without a tie and the first two buttons undone, I'm not sure how long I had been in that daze all I remember is Terrence calling my name then pulling on my arm. "Yes Terrence I'm ready" I said to him as I snapped back from my daydream. He had a weird look on his face, thin within seconds he held the two ties up and said "Let me ask the question again, which one do you like?" I was taken by the question, for one I was thinking of Chad and for two I figured he would have had it all figured out by now. "My bad sweetie, I thought you were saying that you were ready to leave. As far as the tie goes, I like the one in your right hand" Leave it to my husband to make a mountain out of a mole hill and this was one of the occasions.

He finally decided to purchase one of the ties and as you could guess it wasn't the one I chose but who cares, it wasn't anything new so it didn't bother me. Leaving the boutique I couldn't help but look in the direction of the shop and noticed the door was open. No one was coming in or out so I wondered why it was propped open. I told Terrence I wanted to stop and make sure everything was ok, I could tell he really didn't want to but he followed anyway as I walked off. Walking up to the door I noticed Chad in the hallway towards the back of the store talking to who look to be the same lady we now know as his ex.

Why was she here again, did I make myself clear about the drama in the store, just as I was about to enter Terrence touched my hand and said "Do you think we should interrupt, they look like they are in a deep conversation?" I snatched away at the thought of not being able to enter what was mine and told him that "The day I can't enter my own store it won't be mine anymore." And with that said I entered.

"Chad can you tell me what's going on" I asked in a voice that demanded attention. "Sicily you know who this is and Michelle this is Sicily's husband Terrence and vice versa" he said voice trembling. She looked at Chad and said they would handle it later, she pushed her way passed Terrence and I and stormed out the door. I looked at Terrence then at Chad. "Care to tell me what the hell was that about and why was she here?" I had never spoken to him in that tone of voice so I can tell be the look on his face he was shocked and a little hurt. The sight of Terrence fidgeting about told me that he was a little disturbed but that was too damn bad at the moment. Before I knew it I apologized to Chad and told him that I was just concerned and didn't need or want any problems surrounding my place of business. He told me that he understood and that she had some unfinished business but he didn't know what and it wouldn't happen again. "Well as long as it doesn't then we are good. Are you going to the event tomorrow night it should be nice? I have a table for the store in case you and a guess wanted to attend. There is no charge for anything. It's all been taken care of." I told him hoping he would show up. He said he wasn't sure but had thought about it and would put more thought into now knowing someone would be there he can talk to.

Before anything else could be said Terrence cleared his throat and directed his attention to Chad "Yes we will be there and would love to have you and a date sit with us at our table." It was sort of funny the way he kept expressing the fact that we were going to be there and our table. Needless to say I still hadn't forgotten about the looks he and Chad's ex were exchanging. You would've thought they knew each other or had seen each other before. I was going to get to the bottom of this before Ms Michelle left town you can bet. Chad told Terrence since he put it that way he would be happy to come and was looking forward to seeing him there but wouldn't be bringing a date and hope it was ok. I laughed so hard inside at the fact they were playing this tit for tat game but it was cute. I told Chad to lock up when he leaves, that we were headed to our room and I would see him tomorrow night. He reached to shake Terrence hand but instead of Terrence responding he put his hand in the small of my back giving me my cue to exit. Once outside I told him how rude I thought he was and walked off before he got a chance to respond. Once inside the room he pulled me close and said he was sorry. He told me it was hard to see me interact with Chad although he works for me and not to mention he feels Chad has feelings for me and he gathered that from the night he caught us in the room. I told him he had nothing to worry about and not to spoil this weekend. We hadn't been anywhere in a long time together so I was looking forward to it.

We decided to shower together and then head for the bed. I had a hair appointment and massage scheduled in the morning and Terrence was going to play a game of golf. It always seemed to help him unwind but I can't recall him ever playing when we were here before. Maybe he knew someone and decided to catch up with them. I kissed him goodnight and fell asleep in his arms. I was glad he didn't want to play, I was too tired and couldn't get what he said about Chad and caring for me off my mind.

The Big Day

I woke to the sound of someone knocking on the door. I reached for my watch and saw that it was almost 9 o'clock. My hair appointment wasn't until 11 and the alarm was set for 10 so who could this possibly be. Terrence was in the shower or so I assumed because I heard the shower running. Peeping through the door I saw that it was room service and they had a table full of goodies. Terrence knows that before we go anywhere with cameras flashing I don't like to eat a full meal so starting off with a full breakfast was a nice gesture. There were strawberry pancakes, scrambled eggs with cheese, bacon and juice. He was really trying and I couldn't resist. I paid the server a nice tip and knocked on the bathroom door. When he didn't answer I stuck my head inside only to find him on the phone in the shower. Tipping in so that I could hear him I heard him tell someone that "she has to make a decision and he was not going to lose his wife to the hired help or to someone that couldn't afford the upkeep" and ended his call. I slipped back out the door and knocked again as if for the first time but this time I got a response. "I'll be out in a minute Sic. Go ahead have a seat." Really didn't need him to tell me to go ahead, knowing how I loved strawberry pancakes and they were sitting in front of me was all I needed to start without him. I poured us both some juice and set his plate how he like it. By the time I was ready to say grace and dig in he was coming out dressed for golf.

"He babe, hope you didn't mind me ordering us some breakfast. I feel like we are in for a big night and wanted my lady to have all the energy she needs in case there are some surprises." Surprises now what the hell was he talking about? What did that mean? Did this joker know something I didn't know or did he have something up his sleeve. Whatever it was it wouldn't spoil my night or breakfast. We ate with little conversation, few giggles here and there, touching bases with our schedule for the day and planned what time we would meet back at the room. The banquet was starting at 8 and the car was picking us up at 7:30 so we didn't want to be late. I was looking forward to my pampering and my time alone. Don't get me wrong I like spending time with my husband but when it comes down to a big event I need some "me time" so I can unwind.

I had my spa appointment first and decided to try the new one out by the lighthouse. I had seen the reviews in the paper and head a few good things about them. The décor was inviting and relaxing. I was greeted at the door by a gentleman that carried mimosa in one hand and shook my hand with the other. He gave me a deep help and my drink and said he hope I enjoy this experience. Nice smooth music was playing throughout the building and there was a mixture of men and women in the waiting area. I followed him to a room in the rear where I was instructed to undress and slip on the robe laying across the chair and someone would be in shortly. Just as I sat on the table my phone started to vibrate. It was Adriane calling to get an update. "Ms. Thang I was just about to get pampered, what do you want and it better be good" I couldn't help but chuckle at the thought of the expression she would have on her face although it was always good hearing from her.

"Well Mrs. Robinson, I found some information on Ms Michelle Jackson and figured you would be interested. Her and Chad was married for eight years, he worked two jobs putting her to school, she became pregnant during their third year of marriage but had an abortion only because it wasn't Chad's but some guy in Atlanta she had an affair with that came out in the open." She then paused for what felt like several minutes. "Sicily I don't think you want to hear this" she said with a change in her voice. I told her to go on and not hold anything back. "Sweetie it goes on to say that she had an affair with the owner of Robinson's Construction out of Atlanta" and there it was in a nutshell. I could hear her calling my name but my body wouldn't let me speak. She went on to say that this was back in 2006. Before I knew it I was on the floor, I couldn't believe what I was hearing or how small this damn world was. That was right around the time I found out my wonderful husband of so many years was having an affair. I found receipts from gifts I never received and lipstick on his collar a few times. The usual stupid mistakes they made, the kicker was the day I drove his truck to work because mine was getting serviced. Adriane and I were having the usual lunch date. Sitting by the window in the restaurant we happened to notice a woman with shades, a scarf over her head and a raincoat putting a note on the truck. While Adriane wanted to go and bomb rush her I told her to just sit and see what happens. She left the note then pulled off. The note read "Enjoyed our night can't wait to be with you again, my body needs you" and there was a lipstick print where she had kissed the note. That was all the proof I needed to confront him of his tacky ass ways and disappearing acts.

Once I confronted him and threatened to leave he promised me that he would end it and there would be no more problems. I never did find out who she was and all he could say about her was that she was having problems with her husband and they met at a bar a few months ago. I never pushed for any more information and he didn't offer. So here we are now and to find out it was Chad's ex-wife, how could that be? I snapped back to Adriane's voice and told her I was going to be okay and this was not going to end how Terrence or Michelle thought. All of the pieces were finally coming together and making sense. Of course Terrence knew what was going on with Chad and I when I was here. This bitch was telling him everything, she or he or both were the one following me but which one tried to run over Chad? All of a sudden the thought of a massage was the last thing on my mind. I needed to find out if the Terrence had rented a vehicle that weekend of Chad's accident so I called the credit card company and asked for all transactions surrounding those dates. The man on the other end of the phone told me of a car rental the night before Chad's mishap and was returned that evening. So there it was in black and white. There was one more thing puzzling me, could Chad have known who Terrence was and went after me as revenge or a little payback for himself? This I didn't know but was willing to find out and right now.

I decided to call Chad and ask him to meet me by the on the pier. I was really pushing for time with my hair appointment being an hour away but I needed these answers. My heart wouldn't leave me alone. Someone how he managed to be there in 15 minutes, I had a lot going through my mind and only he held the key. He showed up wearing a pair of jeans and a baby blue jersey. As usual he was looking good but that was beside the point. "Sicily you sound like something was wrong, is everything ok" his voice was the calm but a sign of worry. Lord this was going to be a hard pill to swallow if he says yes. I needed to stay focused so I looked out on the water trying to keep from looking into his beautiful deep eyes. By the time I was at the end of all I had found out and about the call from Adriane his head was in his hands covering his face. Was this his way of saying he knew who I was and he had a motive? I sure hoped not because my moments with him had been memorable and my feelings for this man were true. I thought I knew him, I felt I knew him and was this the moment I was going to find out all of this was a lie. I took a deep breath then turned to face him.

With anger in my voice I finally spoke "Chad Jackson please don't sit here and tell me that you knew who I was and that Terrence was my husband" and with that being said the tears begin to flow. What was I doing? Why was I crying over this man? Could it really be love I felt for him or betrayal? My heart was breaking and the tears I couldn't control. What could he possibly say to make this right, nothing at all? I couldn't handle this so I turned to leave. The touch of his hand on my shoulder made me stay. "Baby please don't cry, you know I can't stand it" he said wiping my eyes and pulling me close. "Sicily when I came to Savannah I promise you I had no idea who you were or who you were married to. I was looking for a change, a new start and your ad just happened to be what I needed. I know this may seem hard to believe but I really didn't know and I hope you can find it in your heart to believe that." The look in his eyes told me he was being sincere and he meant every word that he spoke. "I needed a job and you needed a manager, what happened along the way I didn't plan but then again can you really plan love" did this man say love or was I hearing things? As I stepped back to look at him, he held on to my hands and said what I wanted to hear. "Sicily I love you and I can't hold that in anymore. I need and want you in my life. I know you are married but I also know you are not happy. Let me make you happy, let me be all you need and more. I want to continue to be that shoulder to lean on, let me welcome your mornings and end your good nights because trust me I would make sure they were all good." I couldn't believe what I was hearing. I heard him and saw his mouth moving but I couldn't believe it.

"Chad it couldn't work, I am busy and always on the go. My family my boys are in Atlanta and being this far in high school I couldn't dare move them. As far as my husband and the mess he is in right now I am going to handle that but it would be hard for this to work" did I say that? Isn't this the same man I was just crying over because I was afraid he had lied but now that he was pouring his heart out and telling me he loves me was I really going to turn him down and throw away happiness? Before I knew it his lips were on mine and his arms were holding me tight. We kissed for a long time but with all of my strength I was able to pull away. I asked him what did he think we were going to do with our partners in crime and he said not to worry that he would handle everything. We kissed one last time before departing and with that I was headed to my now late appointment.

As I arrived back to the room Terrence was there getting dressed and drinking cognac as he normally did before we went out on the town. He had no idea how special this was going to be. Boy was he in for a surprise. "Sweetie I will be ready to go in less than an hour, I love your suit." Although I was pissed he really did look good in the suit. One thing about him he was a sharp dresser and I loved it.

From the look on his face as I entered the room I could tell he was very pleased at the way I was dressed. I had chosen a black and white gown that fit me perfect, one shoulder tied at the neck and cut low in the front. Just because I was full figured didn't mean I wasn't sexy. "Oh my goodness baby you look amazing" he said in a whisper. I told him thank you as he met me with a kiss. We did the cheek think to keep from smearing my lipstick. The phone rang with notice of the car waiting down stairs. On our way I decided to check my phone. I hadn't looked at is since I called Chad and wanted to make sure I hadn't missed a call. To my surprise there were two missed call. One from Adriane and one from Chad, there was also a voicemail which I decided I would listen to later.

It All Comes Out

As we pulled in front of the building lights were bright and lots of people were standing out talking and being nosey. Some faces were familiar and some not. The door opened and a hand reached in for mine. To my surprise it was Chad and right behind him was Ms. Michelle herself. "Hello Sicily and Terrence. I called you earlier to let you know I had asked Michelle to come and was hoping you wouldn't mind." As I turned to look in her direction she was all smiles and sort of smirking at me but I wasn't gonna let that bother me. I had trust in Chad and if he said he was going to handle it then he was going to do just that. We walked inside all coupled up talking as if nothing was wrong and we were having the best of times. As we sat to the table I couldn't help but notice the look Terrence and Michelle gave each other. It took me back to the same look they gave each other at the boutique. They smiled at each other and I thought I saw this heffa wink but I wasn't sure. Chad had made sure he sat across from me and kept me in his eye sight. It gave me a feel of confidence but then again he always did.

The guest speaker gave his speech and began handing out awards. I wasn't surprised when we got one the shop has really been talk of the town. I said thank you to the audience and also for the hard work my crew had done this year and also welcomed Chad to Savannah and to the family. Once back at the table Chad thanked me for the welcoming and took a look at the plaque. The gaze we gave each other must have been a little too much because Terrence stood up and pulled me by the arm to a corner in the room. His body movements and gesture told everyone that we were arguing or at least he was upset. He asked me what the hell was going on with me and Chad and if we were still fooling around. He had some damn nerve with Ms Bad Weave over at the table. I tried to explain it was nothing because I really didn't know what Chad had in store and I didn't want to spoil it. I told him things were fine, he was making a scene and that I was going back to the table whether he followed or not.

Once back at the table I saw that someone had taken the initiative to order drinks. Chad said he felt that we all could use one to help end the night. Just as Terrence took a sip Chad begin telling a story. "You know there are times in life when you think you have found the perfect jewel, one unlike any other. You do all you can to please them but somehow they manage to slip away out of your life but if you are lucky that opportunity will come back around like new." Terrence sighed as if he could care less. I was listening closely because I knew what we shared and Michelle was sitting there with this same stupid grin she had outside. He went on to say that having the opportunity to love twice was not luck but a blessing. Just then Michelle turned to him and said "Baby I never knew you felt like that, I feel the same and it will be different this time" and leaned in for a kiss. Before her lips reached his he put his hand up to block her, pushed her back and said "You must be joking, did that one drink go to your head that fast, I am talking about Sicily." I turned in my seat to look at Terrence who was choking on his drink. I wanted to laugh.

Chad stood to the head of the table and pulled me to him. He looked at them both and told them of how we figured everything out. That they could rekindle what they had, he told Terrence he knew it was him that tried to run him over that day, that he knew all of his information was coming from this evil ass Michelle. He told her that he knew she was the one that damaged my car. "Terrence I never knew you could be so evil and so damn heartless. All I have stood by you with and this is what I get. You let someone from your past mess up our future. Well I am leaving with Chad and will have your things packed by the time you make it home. I won't tell the boys what you have done it will be up to you" I said with a straight face. If it wasn't for Chads hand on my back I really don't think I could have said it that calm. We then walked out hand in hand smiling as we left, only this time we had each other.

Chad figured it would be best if we got a room somewhere neither of them would think of. More of his budget he said with a joking manner and we both laughed. We made love that night as if it was the first time the passion was fulfilling and well needed. He gave me what I had been longing for and I gave him the same in return. He promised me that things might seem crazy at first but would smooth out and I promised him I would file for a divorce first thing Monday morning.

How We Got Here

I wanted to stop and check on the boutique the following morning. There were some papers we needed and Chad wanted to make a deposit. We were making plans for the coming week, to get a real get away from all the mess and also start planning our future together. We were so caught up in each other making passes and giving kisses. It was like a high school crush and it felt good. I guess letting our guard down was the wrong thing to do, not to mention leaving the front door unlock. I've heard it said there is nothing like a woman scorn, lets just say we now can add a man to that saying.

"Did you really think you were going to take my wife" we both jumped at the sound of Terrence's voice and looked quickly down the hall. He was standing there pointing a gun in our direction and low and behold Michelle was standing behind him. "Terrence what are you doing, put that gun down before you hurt someone!" I tried to be calm but my voice was shaking terribly. I tried to walk toward him but Chad snatched me back with one tug. Terrence then pointed the gun away from me and at Chad. "You see brotha, I would dare hurt my wife, I love her and she is my life but for you to handle me the way you did last night and walk away with her I will kill you with no problem. Matter of fact I am going to kill you and frame her" was he serious? Mama always said you never really knew someone til you pissed on them and she was right. I could've never seen this coming.

"Baby don't do this, let's talk about this" I begged but it was no use because Terrence was coming down the hall with the gun still pointed at Chad. Not sure what was going to happen I stepped in front of Chad and told Terrence I was not going to let him shoot Chad. He then said he would shoot us both and make it look like a murder suicide, then went into detail of writing a note explaining it all. He forced us back into the office pulling me to the side and pushing Chad in a chair. Not thinking I grabbed the umbrella behind the door and hit his hand with it. The gun slid under the desk and the two of them begin to fight. My mind went quickly to Michelle who was walking away. I ran down the hall to get her but she was out the door before I could catch up. Out of nowhere I heard the gun go off. Running back to the office they both were on the floor, Terrence on top of Chad.

"Chad, Terrence, somebody say something please" I screamed at the top of my lungs. I reached over and pulled the panic button on the alarm. As the operator came over the speaker box I told her I needed an ambulance and the police. "Sicily get him off of me please" was what I heard Chad say as he tried to move. As I rolled Terrence over I couldn't help but notice he had been shot in the abdomen. He was breathing but not responding. Crying helplessly I was glad Chad was ok but upset Terrence had been shot. He was hurt and although it was over between him the love was still there. We had a past and children and not to mention happy times.

Helping Chad to his feet I heard the police enter and told us to be still until they reached us. He asked what happened and although we explained everything he still said they would have to arrest Chad until it was all straightened out. The ambulance was loading Terrence up to rush him off and a police car was leaving with Chad. One of the officers asked me a few more questions, I explained everything again and then told him that there is a camera system throughout the store and they could have the tape but I must go to the hospital.

The nurse at the desk told me to have a seat and that a doctor would be out soon to inform me. Hours after waiting I decided to call the boys and tell them what happened before news got to Atlanta. I also called Adriane and asked her to get the boys and come as soon as possible. Hanging up the phone I noticed Michelle coming to the waiting area in tears. Sympathy for her I had none. "Sicily I never meant to cause you any trouble. I messed up my marriage, fell in love with a man I couldn't have even carrying his child but in the end he loved you more." She told me she was going to wait to see if Terrence was ok if I didn't mind and of course I didn't.

Another hour passed then the doctor came out and said that the bullet had been removed and he was going to be ok he would have a few scars where they removed it and would be sore for a while but everything looked good. I asked if I could see him for a few minutes. The doctor told me that he was awake but groggy and not to stay long. I walked to the side of his bed with tears in my eyes. "Sicily I want to apologize for all I have done to you and I will make it right if you let me" he said as if there was going to be a chance for us. I know you are to forgive and that I will do but I won't be able to forget for a while. "Terrence I am so sorry things happened this way also but you have kept a lot from me and I can't let that go. You even tried to hurt Chad and were willing to frame me. I'm filing for a divorce first thing tomorrow. I am going to continue my life with Chad and be happy I just pray you can move on and do the same." I pulled my ring off my finger and laid it on the bed while walking out.

Heading to my car while calling the police station at the same time I almost didn't hear Chad coming behind me, "hey beautiful going my way" he said smiling bright and eyes sparkling. "Sure" I told him as I grabbed him and went in for a kiss. He told me the tape saved him it showed the police everything and he was released with no charges. I told him I ended things with Terrence and I was all his. "That's all I need to know, I got it from here."

And Now . . .

Here we are three years later, the boys have graduated and out of the house. They decided to go to school in Jacksonville with Randall. It made me feel good to know they would be together again and would look after each other. We sold the house and split the money. I moved to Savannah to be closer to my favorite boutique and the man I love. We've been married for a year now and all is well. Terrence is still in Atlanta living in a new condo and business is good for him as usual. For almost a month Chad would get phone calls where someone would hold the line then hang up but they eventually stopped. As for Michelle I haven't seen or heard from her since we were at the hospital. I still have moments when I feel I am being watched but I guess that goes with the game. I was once told love will get you hurt but I say it's the mistreatment of love and not knowing the true meaning that will get you hurt. Love, true love doesn't hurt, it has its moments but it shouldn't hurt. It's one of the most amazing feelings there is and you can quote me on that . . . Mrs. Sicily Jackson.